CRYSTAL LAKE CHRISTMAS

A HOLIDAY NOVEL

BOOK THREE – CRYSTAL LAKE SERIES

Susan W. Green

ISBN: Paperback 979-8-9853114-2-6
ISBN: eBook 979-8-9853114-3-3

Michele Chynoweth, Editor
Design and publishing assistance by The Happy Self-Publisher.

This is a work of fiction. Names, characters, places, and incidents are products of the author's imagination or fictitiously created. All characters are fictional, and any similarity to people living or dead is purely coincidental.

DEDICATION

This book is dedicated to the memory of the wonderful holiday traditions originally crafted by my mother, carried on by my loving family throughout the years, and now passed down to the next generation. May they always be as memorable as they have been over the past seven decades of my life. Christmas truly is the most wonderful and magical time of the year, when anything is possible.

Merry Christmas and Happy Holidays to all!

CHAPTER ONE

December 1st

The sound of the train running over the tracks created a hypnotic rhythm that lulled Kate into a false sense of calm. She finally relaxed her shoulders and slid back into her seat to get more comfortable.

Her thoughts were a jumbled mess of images and emotions that ran the gamut from happy memories to painful heartbreak. She would be better off if she could only focus on the happy times, put the painful memories behind a door, and lock it shut. But she couldn't seem to accomplish the task. The hurt and pain pushed forward, her heart rate increased, and the cycle started all over.

The reality of the situation hit her again, and she could feel the tears forming in her eyes. Before she could grab a tissue, a single tear slowly slid down her cheek. She caught it before it rolled off her chin.

Stop it. You promised yourself no more tears. Kate dug her sunglasses out of her purse to hide her red-rimmed eyes. Since the sun was shining, she could easily get away with the camouflage.

Looking at Kate Taylor Moore from the outside, you'd see an attractive woman in her early sixties, although she seemed several years younger. She was slender, with light brown hair and large brown eyes. Some called her eyes "doe eyes"—big and round like a beautiful deer. Her daughter, Cassidy, had the same gorgeous eyes. Recently, though, Kate's eyes were red more often than not.

Kate worked hard to stay in shape, had a personal trainer, and naturally possessed an excellent sense of style. Of course, it didn't hurt that her late husband, Duncan, had spoiled her, and that she shopped at high-end couture stores in New York City.

Forty years ago, Kate's first husband unexpectedly passed away, and she was left with two small daughters to raise. This ingrained in her the need to be frugal. She was known for finding bargains and being astute in identifying contributions for the charitable organizations she supported. It was hard to say no to Kate.

Vaguely aware someone was speaking to her, Kate looked up and saw the first-class attendant standing next to her seat.

"Hello, Mrs. Moore. I wanted to see if you had completed your lunch order preference. We'll be serving your meal in a few minutes. What can I get for you?" the attendant asked pleasantly.

"No, I haven't filled it out yet, but let me take a quick look." Kate looked at the options and decided the chicken salad sandwich on a croissant would do. She gave the attendant her order and requested a refill of her coffee.

Looking at her watch, Kate was surprised to see that it was almost noon. Where had the time gone this morning as she made her way to Portland, Maine? When she decided to travel by train, she was disappointed to learn there wasn't a direct train between New York City and Portland. Still, she could get as far as Boston and then transfer to a train that would take her to Portland, where she'd arranged for a car service to transport her the last two hours of her trip.

Thinking about arriving in the picturesque town of Lakeview, Maine, made her smile. The quaint lakeside village, with its charming shops, wide sidewalks, and well-maintained landscaping, always made Kate feel that everything was right with the world, especially this time of year when every store window was decorated with Christmas decor.

Lakeview also held fond memories of happier days. She hoped there were more to come. Her daughter owned a gorgeous inn right on the lake, where she would stay during the Christmas holidays...or until she decided what to do with the next chapter of her life.

Staying at Crystal Lake Inn always made her happy. Her daughter, Cassidy Taylor Burnett, had purchased the rundown inn nearly ten years ago. It had been a crumbling mess, and Kate was initially worried that Cassidy had bitten off more than she could chew. But with encouragement from Kate's mother, whom everyone called "Grams," and a strong determination, Cassidy renovated and expanded the inn, and it became a premier attraction for the growing town of Lakeview.

Kate and her second husband, Duncan, had always stayed at the inn and enjoyed the views of the lake from the large front windows, the beautifully maintained landscape along the walkways, and the food. Having a former Michelin-star chef on staff guaranteed delicious meals.

When Kate decided to take the train from New York City to Portland, her daughter was not pleased. Cassidy tried hard to convince her mother that she would drive to the city and bring Kate to Lakeview. The discussion had continued for the past few weeks until Kate finally put her foot down.

"Cassidy, I'm a world traveler, capable of navigating the train system from New York City to Lakeview," she'd said in a firmer tone than usual. "Please refrain from coddling me. I appreciate your offer of a ride, but I'd rather take the train to give myself time to leave some of the painful memories behind. I hope to arrive in Lakeview and be better prepared to face my future. I love you dearly, but I'll remain in the city if you insist on being a nursemaid. Are we clear?"

Cassidy finally backed down. Kate truly hoped Cassidy understood that she needed to be strong, stand on her own two feet, and move forward.

The attendant returned to Kate's seat. "Mrs. Moore, here is your lunch and coffee. Can I get you anything else?"

Kate shook her head at the attendant, indicating she didn't need anything.

The attendant added, "We'll arrive in Boston in ninety minutes. I'll come back to collect your lunch tray before then. Please let me know if I can help you with anything."

As the attendant disappeared into another train car, Kate took out her napkin and bit into her sandwich. She was pleasantly surprised by its fresh taste, though she doubted it had been made on the train. Still, it was delicious, and she suddenly felt hungry, remembering her early start that morning when she'd only had coffee. She had planned to have breakfast on the train, but when she settled into her seat, she got lost in her thoughts.

Once Kate finished her lunch, she made her way to the bathroom, which wasn't easy, considering the constant rocking back and forth of the train cars. Using the seats along the aisle, she steadied herself and safely made her way to the facility. She washed her hands, pulled lipstick from her purse, and tried to apply it without ending up looking like a clown.

Safely seated again, Kate organized her belongings in preparation for the change of trains in Boston. The station, more commonly known as South Station, was a bustling hub for Amtrak. She had prearranged for assistance from the Red Caps upon the train's arrival. She was slightly concerned about the short time frame between arriving in Boston and the departure of her next train to Portland, but with the help of the Red Caps, she felt confident she could navigate the station and get settled on the next train.

As was typical, when a train arrived at the station, there was a mad rush to exit. Kate had learned from past train travel to be ready to bolt as soon as the train came to a stop. She gathered up her belongings and headed to the door.

She felt fortunate she could travel first class, which allowed her to avoid some confusion and not worry about her luggage. A Red Cap was waiting for her as she disembarked, and they swiftly navigated into the station, onto a luggage elevator, and to the next train platform. She was glad when they closed the doors. It was freezing outside, and while the inside of the station was warm, the air on the platform was cold.

Within fifteen minutes of getting off one train, she was seated on the next headed to Portland. Kate quickly stowed her belongings and found her seat located at the front of the train car.

Not sure where the train had originated, she was surprised only a few empty seats remained. She hoped the seat next to her would stay empty. She didn't want to be rude to anyone, but wasn't in the mood to chat.

Kate saw the attendant approaching and pulled out her ticket. "Are we on schedule to arrive in Portland around four o'clock? A car service is picking me up, and they asked that I confirm my estimated arrival time."

"Yes, we are on schedule," the attendant said. "I'll be back in a few minutes to take your drink and snack order."

The attendant quickly moved to the next row of seats. Kate hoped that meant no one would sit next to her. She pulled a new historical romance novel from her purse and placed it on the empty seat. It was a good time to start the book and keep her mind busy. She didn't want to fall into the trap of letting sad memories control her thoughts again.

She was always excited when she started a new book, wondering where the story would take her. She reread the back cover, reminding her why she'd selected it. The backdrop of the novel was a trip to Germany, with tours of several Christmas Villages and the main character getting stuck in a blizzard. A smile formed on Kate's face as she thought it was more likely she would get caught in a blizzard going to Maine than the woman in the book traveling around Germany.

Her thoughts wandered back several years to when Duncan had surprised Kate with a two-week trip across Germany to visit dozens of Christmas Villages. She'd loved every one of them. She recalled that Duncan ended up carrying an armful of bags back to their hotel. He never complained about her shopping or how long it took her to decide on gifts for her loved ones. He was a patient man when it came to Kate, and she adored him for it.

Of course, thinking about the fond memories brought back the dull pain in her chest. Maybe it wasn't so much a pain as an empty space where Duncan had previously lived for the past twenty-five years. Once he died of a massive heart attack, that space was now an aching void.

Her thoughts were interrupted when she heard the attendant speaking to someone. "Here's your seat, sir. We can place your bags on the shelf at the front of the car. That will make it easier for you when we arrive in Portland. I'll return with the coffee you ordered in a few minutes."

Kate heard the man thank the attendant. As soon as she heard the voice, she instantly knew who her new seat partner was. His voice was familiar to her, especially since they'd been friends for almost forty years.

As the attendant helped the new passenger stow his luggage, Kate had a few minutes to reflect on her history with Thornton Reed.

Kate and Thornton met in college. They dated a few times, but mainly, they were part of a group of young adults who'd attended sporting events and concerts and frequented the local hangouts. At one point, Kate thought Thornton might be interested in her romantically, but he had never acted on it. Then, she fell in love with another man, married right after college, and had two daughters, Cassidy and Jennifer.

She barely saw Thornton again for the next decade until her first husband passed away from a massive stroke, leaving her with two young children to raise.

Her family and friends had rallied around Kate during this difficult time, but she was in shock and not coping well with the day-to-day pressures of being a single mother. Grams moved in with Kate to help raise the girls. Her mom saw Kate shutting herself off from everyone and hiding at home. To help her move on, Grams volunteered Kate to serve on the board of Lakeview Memorial Hospital.

Begrudgingly, Kate stepped up to help raise funds for a new wing of the hospital. Looking back, she owed her mother a great deal for her happy life over the past two decades. While on the board, she met her Prince Charming, Duncan Moore. After a whirlwind romance, they married, and Duncan became a wonderful father figure to her two daughters.

Duncan was an excellent provider. As the CEO of Moore Investments, he enjoyed surprising Kate with spontaneous gifts, arranging amazing trips, and spending quality time with the family in Lakeview.

Fast-forward, Kate found it unbelievable now that she was once again in a similar situation —a widow. Now, at age sixty-three, she was trying to put the pieces of her life back together. It felt like a complicated puzzle, yet there wasn't a picture on the top of the box to follow, and a dozen pieces were missing. Her view of the future was at best fuzzy.

Duncan had been gone for over two years, and she still struggled to come to terms with it. She often woke up in the mornings and rolled over to tell him something or to ask about plans for the day. Kate wondered if she would ever feel normal again. At this point, she wasn't even sure she knew what "normal" felt like anymore.

Tears started to fill her eyes once more, but Kate was abruptly pulled out of her trip down memory lane, as there was movement near her seat.

Taking another glance at Thornton's profile, she noticed he had aged well. His sandy-blond hair from his youth was now peppered with gray. He still dressed more professionally than most travelers on the train, and it was clear he took his physical fitness seriously, especially for his age.

As he sat down in his seat, he looked her way. At the same time, Kate looked his way, and they both started laughing.

"Well, well, well. What are the odds of the two of us ending up on the same train bound for Portland? Hello, Kate."

"Hello, Thornton. I'd say the odds were very slim, but I feel lucky since we're both here and seated beside each other. I think I'll play the lottery today." Kate smiled. "How are you? I thought you always drove from the city to Lakeview. What are you doing on the train today?"

"Slow down, Kate. One question at a time." Thornton chuckled. "I'm headed to Lakeview to meet with your son-in-law, Jack, regarding his next book. My condo association is replacing some pipes, and I need to be out for a few days, so it seemed like the perfect solution to enjoy time at Crystal Lake Inn and meet with Jack. We discussed him coming to New York City and meeting me at Patterson Publishing, but we'd both have to stay in a hotel, so going to Lakeview was the better option."

Thornton paused to put his cell phone on the table. "I had some business in Boston and decided it made more sense to take the train to Boston, finish up my business there, and then hop back on the train and continue to Portland. I have a rental car waiting for me in Portland. I'll need it to get around while I'm in Lakeview."

"I'm happy you didn't pull Jack back to the big city," Kate responded. "He seems very happy in Lakeview, and he and Cassidy are up to something. They haven't shared what it is, but they've said it's a surprise for Christmas, and that I'll be thrilled. Knowing the two of them, it could be anything. They are known to go all out for the holidays."

Looking thoughtful, Thornton asked, "Kate, what are your plans for getting from the Portland train station to Lakeview?"

"I've hired a car service. Why do you ask?"

"I have a rental car waiting for me in Portland. Why don't you ride with me? It would be great to have company on the two-hour drive. I'd consider it a favor if you said yes. Once I get off the interstate, that long stretch on US Route 3 seems to drag on forever. We can use the time to catch up. What do you say?"

Kate was hesitant at first. *Do I really feel like making small talk for hours? Then again, it will beat wallowing in this never-ending stretch of sadness.*

Before he could say anything else, Kate replied with a smile. "Yes, I'd like to ride with you. Let me call the car service and cancel my reservation. I'd appreciate the company."

Kate picked up her phone, called the car service, canceled her reservation, and considered calling Cassidy to tell her that her plans had changed slightly. However, she reminded herself she was trying to reduce the amount of hovering her daughter was doing. It was best to leave it alone. She should still arrive around the same time, so why bother Cassidy with an update?

Wanting to avoid specific painful topics, Kate steered the conversation to safer ones, such as what hot bestsellers Patterson Publishing was working on, recommendations for any holiday feel-good fiction, and news of friends they had in common.

Kate easily handled these safe conversation pieces. What she couldn't handle was opening herself up to painful topics, especially with Thornton, who she knew had also had his share of heartache over the past several years. Controlling the conversation was something Kate had mastered, and it usually helped keep her emotions under control—or at least pretend they were.

Several hours later, Thornton and Kate were in the rental car and on their way from Portland to Lakeview. It was winter, and the sun was hiding behind the taller buildings as dusk settled around them.

"Kate, would you like to stop for dinner before we reach the inn? I missed lunch, and my stomach is rumbling. I know a lovely little restaurant about halfway between Portland and Lakeview. What do you think?"

"That sounds wonderful. I had lunch earlier, but it might be too late to eat dinner by the time we get to Lakeview. Of course, Cassidy will have everyone running around, making sure I have a meal. If we stop along the way, I can avoid some of the hovering once I get to the inn."

"I guess that's one good point of never having had children. No one hovers, although sometimes it might be nice if I did have someone to share things with again."

Kate was surprised to hear Thornton mention he might be open to another romantic relationship. She certainly wasn't and didn't plan to be ever again. She couldn't risk another major heartbreak.

Forty-five minutes from Lakeview, they stopped at a lovely seafood restaurant high on a cliff above a harbor. They were seated next to big windows which overlooked the marina below. Due to the winter season, only a few boats were docked.

After the couple settled in, they placed their order with the waiter and were served a basket of freshly baked bread at their table. Kate could smell the yeast in the rolls and couldn't resist them. She took a roll from the basket, bit into it, and set the remaining piece on her bread plate. "I'm glad there are so many lights around the dock. Even in the dark, I can see the boats and some of the small village. I'm sure I've been here before, but I don't recall when. I remember a bookstore, a coffee shop, and a few small retail businesses on the main street. I bet it's a nice place to stroll in warmer weather."

"I'll have to remember to bring you here when the weather is nicer. It would be relaxing to have a good meal and then stroll around the town." Thornton paused. "Although I don't know how often I'll be able to get out of the city."

Their dinner was served, and it was delicious. They declined coffee and after-dinner drinks but agreed to share a decadent-looking piece of chocolate cake. "It's worth every calorie." Kate savored her last bite. "It's absolutely delicious."

Kate suddenly sucked in her breath. "Oh, look, it's starting to snow! Maybe we should get going. I didn't see any mention of snow in the Lakeview forecast for this entire week, but you never know about the weather in Maine this time of year."

By the time they got back on the highway, the snow had already covered the road, but it was light and fluffy, quickly blowing off the surface as they drove through it.

The last few miles to the inn, Kate reflected on her forty-year friendship with Thornton. For years after college, their old group would get together socially every few years. But after he married his now ex-wife, Isabella, their meetings became less frequent and were mainly limited to fundraisers or city events. Kate always felt Isabella was jealous of her and Thornton's easy-going friendship.

Thornton had reentered her life when her son-in-law, Jack, became a bestselling novelist and was represented by his company, Patterson Publishing. She felt fortunate to have several close friends who supported her through life's trials and tribulations, especially Thornton. Kate knew he was always there if she needed him. They shared an unspoken bond, and he understood how deeply she was grieving the loss of her husband.

Kate suddenly realized she was glad they would see each other while he stayed at the inn. Over the past few hours, she'd felt less tormented by her memories. Perhaps their friendship could help her forge a new path to healing. It was time to stop letting the pain dominate her thoughts and her life. Duncan would always hold a special place in her heart, and the memories would remain, but she had to move forward and live her life to the fullest. That is what Duncan would have wanted—and what she desperately needed.

CHAPTER TWO

December 2nd

The following morning, the bright sun reflected off the snow that had fallen the previous evening. Even after Kate and Thornton arrived at the inn, the snow had continued to fall for several hours, leaving four inches on the ground. It would probably stick around for a few days since temperatures were expected to be in the mid-twenties, but the roads would be cleared quickly. It was Maine, and snow was something they dealt with on a routine basis.

As soon as Kate opened her eyes, she saw the sunlight through the tiny slit in the curtains. She got up and walked over to the window, pulled the curtains back, and admired the stunning view of the snow-covered lake. It was easy to see why the inn was typically fully booked, even during the cold winter months.

Kate settled into the overstuffed chair strategically placed by the large double windows to get the best view of the lake. She needed time to reflect on the chaotic greeting she and Thornton received when they arrived at the inn the previous evening. Being prepared to handle Cassidy's questions was the best way to minimize the inquisition her daughter had started as soon as she and Thornton stepped through the door. Thankfully, Kate had been able to postpone the discussion until this morning.

Typically, Cassidy was a level-headed and easy-going person. However, she was known to go overboard in organizing everything, which often extended to trying to manage everyone's lives as well.

Since Duncan's passing, Kate had become the focus of Cassidy's overprotectiveness and hovering. On one hand, Kate appreciated her daughter's love when she needed it most, but over the past two years, Cassidy seemed to have taken on the role of the parent.

Kate replayed the entire scene from the prior evening in her mind, trying to prepare herself for the inevitable and uncomfortable confrontation waiting for her downstairs.

When Kate had walked into the inn the prior evening at ten o'clock with her coat covered in snow, the group watching her appeared tense. Among them were Cassidy, her husband, Jack, and the inn's chef, Peter Cooper, along with his wife, Amanda, who helped manage the inn.

Cassidy still looked beautiful even though she was clearly upset. Her slender body was ramrod straight as she stared at her mother with those big, doe-like eyes, flicking her long, light brown hair behind her shoulders. Cassidy was a force to be reckoned with. As a business owner and active member of the Lakeview Town Council, she usually took charge of stressful situations.

Her husband, Jack, the typical introverted author, as usual, was happy to step back and let his wife lead, especially when it came to Cassidy's overprotectiveness of her mother. Since Jack had a strong, muscular physique, people were often surprised when he let Cassidy take charge. Kate tried to contain her grin, seeing her handsome son-in-law also stare at her with his big blue eyes.

Cassidy was the first to speak, her arms folded across her chest. "Where have you been, Mother? I expected you two hours ago, and with the unexpected snow, I was worried. I was ready to call our local Chief of Police to look for you." Cassidy suddenly noticed Thornton walking in behind her mother, carrying several suitcases. "And why are you with Thornton? I'm confused."

Kate took a deep breath. "Well, hello, everyone. I'm sorry if I worried you. Thornton and I ended up on the same train and decided to share a ride. We stopped to eat since I figured we'd miss dinner, and we didn't want you fussing about us. We had a lovely meal on the way. I guess we took longer over our dinner than we realized. I'm sorry if I worried anyone."

Kate walked over to her daughter, Cassidy. "Give me a hug. I'm so happy to be here." Kate went around hugging everyone gathered in the lobby. "It's been a long day. Do you mind if I settle into my room now, and we can talk in the morning? I'm exhausted."

Amanda and Peter had immediately said goodnight and went to their apartment on the other side of the kitchen. As soon as they closed the door behind them, Amanda said, "I'm glad Cassidy and Kate agreed to postpone their discussion until tomorrow. I don't want to be around when Cassidy tries to 'mother' her mother and Kate plays the typical 'parent' role.

Amanda had gone to college with Cassidy and their other best friend, Trish. She was the tallest among them, with hazel eyes and sunlit light brown hair. Amanda carried herself with an air of sophistication and came from a wealthy family in New York City, but preferred the quieter life of Lakeview. When she first moved from the city to the charming New England town, her family wasn't happy with her decision. However, over time, especially after the birth of their daughter, Emma, her parents realized how happy she was, and they repaired their relationship, visiting Lakeview several times a year.

Although Peter was a Michelin-starred chef, he favored life in Lakeview and enjoyed crafting tasty meals at the inn. The nearby water provided frequent chances to sail his fifty-foot boat. Summer days spent on the boat deepened his tan, complemented his blond hair, and made his sea-blue eyes stand out. By any standard, he was a very handsome man.

Peter reached over and pulled his wife into an embrace, "You know you'll get an earful from Cassidy in the morning.

Kate doesn't stand a chance of her daughter not hovering over her. If you think about it, Cassidy hovers over all of us."

Agreeing to Peter's statement, Amanda grabbed her husband's hand and headed down the hall to their bedroom to check on their two-year-old daughter, Emma. She was sleeping peacefully, as she had been for the past two hours, yet they constantly watched her from the baby monitor on their phones. She was their pride and joy.

Meanwhile, Jack helped Thornton take the luggage upstairs to their rooms.

Jack stopped at Thornton's door, "Good night, my friend. I'm sorry about the way Cassidy acted when you arrived. She's been worried about Kate lately. I'm hoping the time together at the inn will help Kate figure out her next steps and allow Cassidy to feel more confident her mother will be okay."

Continuing, Jack said, "I felt better when I heard Kate rode with you. I knew she was safe. I wasn't a fan of her using the car service, but she refused to let us pick her up in Portland. I'm not sure who is more stubborn, Kate or Cassidy. Thank you for taking such good care of my mother-in-law. She means the world to all of us."

Jack and Thorton said goodnight, and Jack headed down the hall to drop off Kate's luggage in her room.

Reaching Kate's door, Jack watched as Kate quickly turned to Cassidy, who was following her to her room. "I love you, dear. You're such a good daughter, and I'm excited to celebrate the holidays with all of you here at the inn. Please keep in mind, though, that I'm not here to have a babysitter. Give me a hug, and let me get some rest. We'll talk in the morning."

Cassidy, of course, wanted to discuss the situation immediately, but Jack could tell his mother-in-law was tired, so he interrupted.

"Let's postpone this until the morning dear." He gently put his arm around Cassidy, who nodded wearily in agreement,

Cassidy leaned over and hugged Kate. "Alright. Goodnight, Mother. I'll see you at breakfast. "

Kate shook her head to dismiss the scene from last night and refocused her thoughts on this morning. It was her first full day back in Lakeview, and she was determined to answer her daughter's questions while making sure Cassidy understood her need for independence.

She couldn't stay in her room forever. By the time she finished dressing, she felt ready to face her daughter. Well, at least she thought she was prepared.

Her last thought before leaving her room was that Cassidy was acting out of love. Kate also needed to act out of love, but she had to remind her daughter *she* was the parent and fully capable of taking care of herself. No hovering needed.

As Kate headed to the dining room, she paused briefly in the living room to admire the roaring fire in the large fireplace. Crystal globes, brightly lit with candles, sat on each end of the mantel. Sofas and chairs were arranged in a conversational style near the fireplace, while others were positioned by the large front window overlooking the lake.

As she entered the dining room, she observed the tables were adorned with crisp white tablecloths. Mahogany sideboards and glass-front cabinets lined two walls. On the far wall, an efficient arrangement of warming trays held the morning buffet, while china and silverware indicated the starting point.

The dining room was crowded, with only a few seats available. Kate quickly grabbed a cup of coffee from the fully stocked coffee bar and sat at a table in the far corner. The dining room was busy, and even though it was winter, each table was decorated with a small vase of fresh flowers. Overall, it felt unexpectedly peaceful. From her seat, she could see across the entire room and admire the beautiful furnishings. As often as she visited the inn, she never tired of the welcoming atmosphere or the stunning lake views.

Kate was still admiring the décor when she was interrupted by someone placing a plate of food in front of her. She looked up and saw Cassidy putting her own plate down at the opposite seat. "Good morning, Mother. I saw you walk into the room, and it was a good time for me to grab my breakfast. I noticed you hadn't gotten yours, so I selected some of your favorites."

"Thank you, Cassidy. Everything looks delicious. Of course, I wouldn't expect anything less with Peter Cooper as your chef. How are Peter, Amanda, and little Emma? I didn't get to say more than hello to them last night when I arrived."

Before Cassidy could say anything, Kate reached across the table and lightly placed her hand on her daughter's. "I was hoping we could talk this morning. I wanted to apologize again for worrying everyone last night. I'll be more considerate during the remainder of my stay, but I also don't want to have to account for every move I make. By the way, you were right. You said leaving the city for a while and coming here might be exactly what I needed. I woke up feeling much more positive this morning. Thank you for caring so much about me, but let's put the hovering to rest. Okay?"

Cassidy looked across the table at her mother. "I understand, and I'll try my best not to hover. You do look better this morning, and you sound more cheerful."

Kate watched her daughter's eyebrows furrow and her big eyes narrow a bit, and knew she was trying to figure something out, so she quickly changed the subject. "I'm eager to hear your plans for the holiday events."

Taking a deep breath, Cassidy replied. "We've never closed the inn for a private family event for more than a long weekend, and there are so many moving parts to wrap up. You know me, I have a spreadsheet with all the little details, but there's still a lot to be done. With multiple families moving here for two weeks, the renovations in Room #210, and coordinating with the events in town, it wouldn't take much to derail everything. I know it will all work out. I'm just overly excited."

Kate sighed with relief, feeling happy her daughter wasn't going to dwell on last night. "So far, you've only shared that you intend to close the inn for the last two weeks of the year and want the family and our closest friends to stay here. That sounds lovely, but most of the people you've mentioned, except for me, live within a ten-mile radius of the inn. What's the plan?"

"Having everyone under one roof will be so much fun. Peter has plans for several special meals, and Amanda has games lined up for all ages. She even bought some silly holiday-themed prizes. We'll have hot cocoa and popcorn by the fireplace and sing songs. And if we get lots of snow, everyone will be right here, safe and sound, so no one will have to worry about traveling in it."

Kate could see there was something else her daughter wanted to tell her. Finally, Cassidy couldn't contain her excitement any longer. "Mother, I have a big surprise for you. Jennifer and her family are finally coming home from Europe!"

Jennifer, Cassidy's younger sister, along with her husband, Michael, and their now six-year-old daughter, Addie, had moved to Europe three years ago. Michael had an exciting job with the U. S. Department of State. It was a great career opportunity for him, and it had the added benefit of allowing the family to travel frequently across Europe. Regrettably, because of the extensive travel and Michael's busy schedule, the family didn't often return to Lakeview.

Kate clapped her hands together. "This is fantastic news. I didn't think they were coming home for another few months. Michael's job extended his stay yet again, and the last time I spoke to Jennifer, she said they wouldn't be home until March. I can't wait to see Addie! Each time I visited, she was taller and smarter, and I was shocked when she spoke to me in at least three different languages. She's benefited from their moving around and experiencing various countries, languages, and cultures. When do they arrive?"

"They should be here on December 8th, but there are so many things they need to get done, including Michael wrapping up his final reports to the Secretary of State. I was thinking how crazy it must be for Jennifer to pack three years' worth of belongings and have their larger items shipped to the States for storage. They will be here for all the fun activities and the Lakeview Christmas Village. I've missed my little sister and her family. I can't wait for Addie to finally meet her cousin, Katie, since they haven't yet met. Katie's been too young for us to take her to visit with them, so this will be a wonderful homecoming for the entire family."

Cassidy stopped to gather her thoughts before continuing. "I've created a calendar for the twelve days of Christmas, with a variety of events either here at the inn or in town. It's a fun-filled two weeks, and I hope everyone will join in. We're all so busy these days that finding quality time together is becoming increasingly difficult. I want this to be a memorable Crystal Lake Christmas."

Kate smiled and asked, "When can I see the calendar? I hope you left me time to finish shopping, wrapping, and reading the new book I bought before I left the city. I've tried starting it twice, but haven't been successful. I also need some quiet time to figure out my next steps."

"Of course, everything is optional, and I know you might not join some of the activities, but it will be fantastic to have you be part of the events where we're all together." Cassidy paused and said, "I have a busy day. I'm finalizing the calendar and have a meeting this afternoon with the contractor, who has finally obtained the permits for renovating the old storage room, also known as Room #210. I can't wait to see his final renderings."

Cassidy shared a few more details with her mother about coordinating with the events that Lakeview held each year, along with a new baking contest they would host at the inn. Peter agreed to be the judge. "And there's excitement about the Lakeview Center for the Performing Arts performance of The Nutcracker. This year it features prima ballerina Karina Celeste DuPree. And, of course, I've reserved 'family time' at the Lakeview Ice Rink, including private lessons from Olympic Gold medalist Abby Roark, who now owns the rink." Cassidy was out of breath, her eyes sparkling.

"You've been extremely busy and creative," Kate remarked to her daughter, trying to convey her pride in what Cassidy was trying to accomplish. "Just hearing about some of the activities is exciting. And Jennifer and her family are coming home! We'll have everyone under one roof. It feels…magical. I can't wait!"

The two women continued discussing the plans while they finished their meal. A server stopped to refill their coffee cups and remove their empty plates.

"Mother, what are your plans for today?" Cassidy asked.

"I've decided to have a quiet day at the inn. I still need to put my things away in my suite and get settled. And I finally want to start reading my new book. It's the perfect way to spend the day, especially after the hectic weeks of closing my condo and saying goodbye to close friends. Plus, yesterday's travel day was tiring. Yes, a quiet day in your beautiful inn is exactly what I need. I think I'll get a to-go cup and take this coffee to my room with me." Kate finished her thought and stood up from the table.

"Mother, you don't need to take that cup with you. I'll have someone bring a fresh pot to your room. Knowing the owner of the inn has some perks. If you need anything, don't hesitate to call me." Cassidy reached over and hugged her mother.

Kate smiled. "Yes, it does pay to know the owner, the manager, and the chef. I appreciate the extra service. Enjoy your day, and I'll see you at dinner." Kate started to walk out of the dining room, but glanced across the room before she left.

She didn't see who she was looking for, and Kate wondered why Thornton had popped into her mind. *Why did I replay our time together from yesterday over and over last night? Why did thoughts of Thornton keep me awake?* She yawned. It was odd.

CHAPTER THREE

December 3ʳᵈ

The temperature was in the low twenties, with a gentle breeze. Cassidy could see her breath and feel the chill on her cheeks as she walked briskly to her favorite coffee hangout, The Perk.

Stepping into the coffee shop, Cassidy took a deep breath and smiled. The aroma of strong, fresh-brewed coffee, mixed with the sweetness of bakery treats, had her stomach rumbling.

As Cassidy waited in the short line, her attention was drawn to the color scheme. Subtle blues and a creamy peach created a calming and inviting effect, precisely what she needed. The past week had been hectic, and she craved a calm respite, especially when it involved strong coffee, sweets, and her best friends.

The customer in front of her paid for his order and walked away. Cassidy moved up to the counter. At the last second, she had a moment of indecision as several options floated through her mind. There were too many tempting sweets in the bakery cabinet. The cashier remained patient and kept a smile on her face.

"Sorry, it shouldn't be this difficult to make up my mind," Cassidy said. "I knew exactly what I wanted when I arrived, but now I'm having trouble deciding. I want to combine my love of strong coffee with something sweet, but I'm not sure I know what that is."

The cashier started to list a few options, but then a "Dalgona" jumped into her brain. It was a combination of strong coffee and deathly sweetness. "Oh, I know, I'll take a Dalgona, please."

The cashier relayed the order to the barista, handed Cassidy a numbered card for her table, and informed her of the price. Cassidy made the payment and stepped out of line. She spotted her friend Trish entering the shop, paused to hug her, and noticed a table becoming available by the front windows overlooking Main Street.

Once Trish had her order, she walked over to the table where Cassidy was already sitting. She was juggling a large coffee mug in each hand while balancing a dessert plate on top of one of the mugs. "Please, take my cheese croissant and set it on the table for me. I should have realized I'm not as coordinated as I think I am, and there's no way I want to drop this beauty. It's still warm from the oven."

"Why do you have two mugs? Are you that desperate for caffeine?" Cassidy asked jokingly.

"Silly girl, one of these is yours. I offered to bring your fancy drink to you and save someone the trouble of bringing it out. What is that delicious-looking concoction?" Trish questioned.

Cassidy smiled. "I'm surprised you don't recognize it. This is the Dalgona our friend Sarah occasionally indulges in. It's to die for. It popped into my mind when I needed strong coffee but also craved something sweet. If I remember correctly, Sarah described the process for making it, saying the barista starts with dark instant coffee, adds water and two heaping spoonfuls of sugar, and then uses an electric mixer to create stiff peaks in the mahogany-brown mixture. It's finished with a dollop of creamy whipped cream and freshly shaved chocolate and caramel bits. There are too many calories to count, but you won't want to miss a drop. I might even lick the mug when I'm done."

"It looks delicious," Trish said as she broke off a piece of her croissant and popped it into her mouth. "Yummy!" She picked up her mug, blew across the top to cool it, and took a deep sip. "This is the perfect way to start my morning."

"Hey, you two! You were so engrossed in your food that you didn't even notice me enter the shop." Amanda set down her mug and then her plate, which held a blueberry muffin. "Cassidy, what's that delicious-looking drink in your mug?"

Trish and Cassidy both laughed. "I just described it to Trish," Cassidy replied. "It's a Dalgona. Sarah calls it the most decadent thing in a mug."

Before Cassidy could say anything else, Amanda interrupted her. "Oh yeah, I recall how Sarah always moaned when she sipped it, and then at the end, she used her spoon to get every last bit of any chocolate that drifted to the bottom. I keep forgetting to try it. On the other hand, it must have two thousand calories, so maybe not."

The three friends spent the next ten minutes catching up on local news and discussing their families.

"By the way," Cassidy said, "Sarah called last night and gave me an update on Tom's broken leg. The doctor said it was a clean break, but he's still out of commission for six weeks. Sarah's running around trying to manage everything she has going on, plus taking care of her husband. It's a good thing his sister, Leah, offered to stay at their house for a few hours every day."

Amanda added, "The biggest issue is that the beautiful Victorian house they bought two years ago and are in the process of remodeling doesn't have a bathroom on the first floor. They had planned to add one with the next phase of the renovations this spring. Tom is frustrated with himself for not doing it before they moved in."

"Yes, but because of that, Sarah finally got Tom to agree to move to the inn and join us for our special Christmas events," Cassidy said excitedly. "The accessible room on the first floor is perfect for Tom's situation, and it also offers a stunning view of the lake and the surrounding forest. With the snow-covered trees right now, it's one of the best views in town. They're moving in tomorrow, and I'm excited to include them in our events."

Cassidy paused and took a deep sip of her Dalgona before continuing, "Tom had a follow-up doctor's appointment this morning, which is why Sarah couldn't join us. I promised to update her later today when she stops by the inn to drop off merchandise for the retail area of the lobby. We continue to sell out of those adorable baby quilts her artisan's group handmakes."

Glancing at her watch, Cassidy was surprised by how much time had passed. She quickly pulled a small laptop from her shoulder bag, indicating she was ready to talk business.

"Today, we need to finalize the plans for the special family and friends event at the inn. I have a name in mind, and I hope you like it. If not, I would appreciate your suggestions. What do you think of Crystal Lake Christmas? We could refer to it as CLC."

Cassidy paused and looked at her friends. "You don't like it, do you?" What are your suggestions?"

Trish and Amanda exchanged glances. "I didn't realize our special time at the inn was going to have its own name," Trish said hesitantly. "From looking at your laptop, it appears to have its own spreadsheet, and—is that a website just for those invited? Oh my, you mean for this to be something truly special, huh? In that case, I say let's go with CLC. It will help keep the CLC events separate from the annual Lakeview Christmas events. Amanda, do you agree?"

"It sounds good to me. Let's see what else you have in mind." Amanda pulled out a notepad and pen from her purse.

Cassidy handed each of her friends a folder containing a thick stack of paper. The first page outlined who was staying at the inn and the rooms to which they were assigned. The following pages were a detailed plan of all activities....

Crystal Lake Christmas (AKA – CLC)

- Crystal Lake Inn - closed to the public after 12/11, when the last guests depart.
- Family and friends check in during the following days.
- Staying at the inn:
    - Amanda, Peter, and Emma Cooper (Suite 110, apartment)
    - Sarah and Tom Spencer (Suite 105, accessible room on the first floor)
    - Cassidy, Jack, and Katie (Suite 200)
    - Kate Moore (Suite 201 and adjoining room 202)
    - Trish and Derrick Williams (Suite 203)
    - Jennifer, Michael, and Addie (Connecting rooms 204 and 205)
    - Dr. Sam Foster, Leah, Ellie, and Elijah (Connecting rooms 206 and 207)
    - Karina Celeste DuPree (Scheduled to depart 12/23, Suite 208)
    - Thornton Reed (Scheduled to depart 12/7, Suite 209). Note: After Thornton checks out, Suite 209 will be the only available room. We'll keep it vacant in case of emergencies.
    - Room #210 – CLOSED FOR RENOVATIONS

The following section listed a long series of departure and arrival dates for those requiring transportation to an airport or train station. Beyond that were pages of details. But you wouldn't expect anything less from Cassidy.

After the women had a few minutes to review the document, Cassidy continued. "The renovations in Room #210 add some challenges to the plan. I wish we had started the project months ago, but it didn't make sense during the high-traffic tourist season. The good news is there are no structural changes, and the contractor has confirmed he will complete the work within two weeks. The bad news is that we have to start cleaning it out this week. I could use some extra help for a couple of days."

Both women said they would be there to help.

Cassidy continued, "My mother offered to help, but under no circumstances do I want her helping us. The room is extremely dusty. Some boxes are falling apart and won't make it to the dumpster, so we'll need to re-box them. If I know my mother, she'll want to sift through every box to see if she can find any treasures. We don't have time for that. We'll quickly look in each box and head to the dumpster. Wear your oldest clothes."

Trish flipped through a couple of pages and stopped when she saw the section detailing the special day of The Nutcracker ballet. "The Nutcracker is my favorite ballet. I first saw it when I was about nine years old, and I was captivated by the ballerinas, the costumes, and the story. I will admit the giant mouse scared me a bit, but I got over that at some point. Well, if I'm being honest, he's still not my favorite character in the ballet." Trish paused. "But I've never met the famous prima ballerina Karina Celeste DuPree. It's exciting she agreed to perform two shows at the Lakeview Center for Performing Arts with dancers from the local dance school. It will be amazing."

Cassidy jumped in, adding, "I don't remember my mother mentioning she knew Karina Celeste until recently. It seems they move in some of the same circles in the city, and since Mother is a patron of the Lakeview Theater, she helped broker the deal when someone heard the ballerina booked an extended stay in Lakeview."

Amanda looked up quickly. "Is it too late for us to get tickets to one of the two performances of the ballet?"

"Mother already bought tickets for everyone staying at the inn during CLC and scored special backstage passes for a meet-and-greet. She refuses to allow anyone to pay her for the tickets. She said it would be her gift to everyone."

Trish looked thoughtful for a moment. "Why would a world-famous ballerina be staying in Lakeview and performing two shows of The Nutcracker? Isn't this time of year typically filled with multiple performances happening every week? I read in the *Lakeview Gazette* that she usually travels the globe, performing in all the major cities. Last year, she received the Prix de Lausanne award, the highest honor in the ballet world. She was the youngest ballerina to receive the honor. I can't connect the dots. Am I missing something?"

Cassidy lowered her voice and confided, "As my mother explained to me, Karina Celeste DuPree, known by her stage name Karina Celeste, is approaching her thirty-fifth birthday. She suffered a foot injury several months ago, and it hasn't healed as quickly as her doctor had hoped. Continuing her performances and the unending hours of practice would cause irreparable damage to her feet. She's struggling to maintain her en pointe movement, and with the impending age at which most prima ballerinas retire, along with her injury, she announced her retirement."

She stopped to take a sip of her Dalgona. "It seems she spent several summers in Lakeview with her family when she was younger, and she holds cherished memories of the town and of staying at Crystal Lake Inn before I purchased it. She decided to perform her last two shows in Lakeview as a special tribute to her parents for their unwavering support throughout her career, as well as to the theater where her love for ballet began. I was genuinely saddened to hear about her retirement, but we're lucky she chose to close this chapter of her career here in Lakeview."

The women continued to discuss the special plans and then headed their separate ways to attend to business, run errands, and try to get everything done during daylight hours. It got dark so early this time of year. They planned to meet again at the inn where Peter was making a hearty stew for dinner.

An hour later, Cassidy finished shopping and was almost back at the inn when she realized she had been mentally running through the spreadsheets while driving, and her car swerved slightly as she careened around a sharp turn. She shook her head to bring her attention back to the road ahead. *Phew, that was close.*

CHAPTER FOUR

December 4th

Thornton and Jack had spent most of the day at Jack and Cassidy's house. Their lakeside cottage had been fully renovated and expanded when their daughter, Katie, was born three years ago. Jack's office was on the second floor, and its prominent feature was a large window overlooking the lake. Thornton understood how inspired Jack felt while writing in his office. Even though Thornton wasn't a writer, he always thought this setup was the perfect place for one.

The two men were engaged in a deep conversation as they entered the inn. Upon stepping inside, they stomped the snow off their boots onto the thick rug and paused in the lobby.

Thornton was about to speak when he heard footsteps on the stairs. He looked up and saw it was Kate.

"Hello, gentlemen. I heard you two were at Jack's today, working on his next bestseller."

Jack chuckled. "I'm hoping it's another bestseller, but you know how fickle the public can be. Personally, I feel like this book is my best yet, but it remains to be seen until we hear from our readers." Jack paused and looked at Thornton.

A smile spread across Thornton's face. "First, Jack has to finish it before we can float it to his group of advanced readers for their feedback. It seems that even the mighty Thomas J. Burnett, AKA Jack, can get stalled on finding the climactic ending his fans have come to expect."

Jack's phone rang. He looked at the screen. "I need to take this call. Please excuse me," he said, walking away.

"Kate, where were you headed when we interrupted you?" Thornton asked.

"I was headed to the library. Cassidy mentioned they had a roaring fire going in the fireplace. I brought my new book and had planned to curl up in one of those big overstuffed chairs near the fire and read."

Thornton followed her into the library, taking a moment to look around. There was indeed a crackling fire. He also noticed the oversized chairs on each side of the fireplace, a sofa, several other chairs, and a small round table with chairs in front of the large windows overlooking the lake. A chessboard was set up on the small table, and it appeared that a game had been underway but was abandoned. He was reasonably good at the game and saw a great move, but decided not to interfere with the board.

"I don't want to interrupt your reading, so I'll head to my room." Thornton hoped Kate would ask him to join her, but when she didn't respond immediately, he reached out and lightly touched her arm as he started to walk past her. He was surprised to feel a slight tingle run up his arm. He looked at Kate and thought he saw surprise register on her face, but she quickly recovered.

Before Thornton could decide what to do next, Peter, the inn's chef, interrupted them.

"Hello, you two. I saw you heading to the library, and I took the liberty of bringing you a cup of hot cocoa." Peter handed Kate and Thornton each a steaming mug.

"Is this the famous cocoa with decadent chocolate, handmade whipped cream, and a secret ingredient you won't share with anyone?" Kate practically purred.

A smile began at the corners of Peter's mouth until his entire face lit up. "Yes, it is, and don't ask for the secret ingredient. It's been handed down from my grandmother with the promise never to share it. Just drink and enjoy. I pulled some chocolate chip cookies from the oven a few minutes ago. Can I bring you some?"

Thornton looked at Kate, and they both declined the cookies. Peter walked back down the hallway and headed to the kitchen.

"Let's sit by the fire and enjoy this delicious cocoa." Thornton walked to one of the chairs and offered to hold Kate's mug until she settled into the other one.

"You are always the gentleman, Thornton. Thank you."

Thornton took a few steps and sat in the chair across from Kate. "So, how has your stay been so far? I haven't seen you since we arrived. Have you settled into what will be your home for the next few months?"

Kate sipped her drink and ran her tongue across her lips. "Yes, I'm all settled in. Yesterday, Cassidy wouldn't leave me alone until she helped me unpack, including arranging some family photos she brought from her house. I feel very comfortable here and don't have to cook my meals or shop for food. It's the perfect set-up."

A smile warmed her face. "And Cassidy had a beautifully wrapped package waiting in my room. It was a handmade lap quilt crafted by the local artisan group. It's a smaller version of the larger quilt that covers the bed. The pattern is called Lone Star. An eight-point star covers the entire top of my bed. With shades of red and green in the star, it's the perfect centerpiece for the other holiday decorations Cassidy arranged in my room."

Thornton, trying to be funny, said, "I'm surprised you don't have a ten-foot tree in your room."

Kate laughed. "Not a ten-foot tree, but there is a four-foot, fully decorated Christmas tree that stands in the corner of the room near the large window. Of course, Cassidy has set a timer for the lights to come on at dusk and turn off at eleven. The coffee setup contains the fixings for hot cocoa. And…there's whipped cream in the small beverage refrigerator. Cassidy thought of everything. It's a Christmas wonderland in my room. I'm quickly getting into the holiday spirit."

Kate's happy and content look quickened Thornton's pulse. He'd been so worried about her for months, and now it looked like she was finally coming out of the fog and looking forward to the holidays.

Thornton couldn't help but return Kate's smile. "The look on your face is priceless. You remind me of a kid talking about Santa coming soon. It makes me happy to see you so excited. By the way, I heard a rumor that Jennifer and her family are coming home sooner than expected. Was that a surprise also?"

"Oh my, yes! The surprises keep coming. Along with all the special events Cassidy has planned for us, the most special one is spending Christmas with my daughters and their families in the same country and under one roof. It's been three years since that happened. As a mother and grandmother, there's no better gift."

"I knew you'd be excited to have your family together for a change," Thornton responded.

"Thornton, what are your plans for the holidays? Jack mentioned that you declined his invitation to join us here at the inn. He said you liked being in the big city during Christmas, as it was deserted and quiet, and a good time to get a lot of work done. You don't mean that, do you?"

His smile faded, and he was quiet for a moment. "When I was married to Isabella, we traveled so much during the holidays. We were constantly in motion. I'm done with all of that. I am truly looking forward to a calm and quiet two weeks. The office is closed, most of my friends will be out of town, and I have a stack of books I need to read. The stack has grown so tall that I'm using it as an end table. Don't worry about me. I'll be fine."

"I don't like it one bit," Kate responded. "You could stay here with us. I heard Cassidy say we have one room available. You should stay."

Thornton knew Kate was sincere about her invitation. He wavered momentarily but didn't think it was a good idea to insert himself so deeply into the family's holiday. "Thank you, Kate, but I need to head back to the city as soon as my condo is ready. The contractor called me earlier and said I could move back on December 7th. So, you'll have me around to bother you for a few more days."

Kate leaned over and touched his arm. "You are always welcome. Keep that in mind."

They drank their cocoa and looked into the fire for a moment.

Thornton was the first to break the silence. "Kate, if you don't mind, can I ask what your plans are for the condo in the city? Or the lovely lake house you and Duncan built here in Lakeview a few years ago? I knew you were temporarily leasing it out, but are you considering moving back this spring when the lease is up?"

"I don't mind you asking. The plans for the lake house are simpler than the condo. If I decide to move back to Lakeview, I'll wait for the current tenant's lease to expire, and I'll move back in. As you mentioned, it's a lovely place with great views of the lake."

Kate paused, and Thornton noticed a distant look in her eyes. "Kate, it's okay. You don't need to talk about your plans for the condo."

She smiled, although it didn't reach her eyes. "As for the condo, when I had everything packed to come to Lakeview, I did a walk-through of the space. I realized it would be too painful to think about it all the time. So, I called my realtor and let them know about the possible sale, but asked them not to take any action until I got back to them. It's a beautiful penthouse with amazing city views. I think it will sell for a good price. Holding onto the condo is only a stalling tactic, but I'm just not ready to sell it yet. I need to move beyond the past and figure out my future. "

Drinking the last of her hot cocoa, Kate set her cup on the table, leaned forward in her chair, and stared into the fire. She looked lost in thought. Thornton decided to follow her lead and remained silent. Maybe Kate wasn't as healed as he had thought earlier in their conversation.

Kate was the first to break the silence again. "Thornton, we've never had the opportunity to discuss your divorce. We both were going through extremely difficult situations at the same time. You seem okay, but between us two old friends, are you truly okay? I hope you don't mind me asking."

Thornton was deep in thought and was startled when he heard Kate speaking to him. Before he spoke, he stood up and pulled his chair closer to Kate's. He felt the need to be closer to her as they shared the past. And it gave him a good reason to get close enough to smell that flowery perfume she was famous for wearing.

Wait… what is wrong with me? Why am I getting closer to Kate to catch a whiff of her perfume? I need to get my head back in the right frame of mind. Slightly shaking his head, he turned toward her but sat up straight.

"I don't mind talking about it. My situation was painful but different from yours. Isabella and I mutually agreed to the divorce. As you know, Isabella's family owns a large international business headquartered in their homeland of Spain. When her father started to have serious health issues several years ago, Isabella spent more and more time in Spain.

I can say one thing for her, Isabella is a savvy and creative businesswoman, and the business started to grow quickly, meaning she spent more time away from New York City. As if our lives weren't complicated enough, I was offered the CEO position at Patterson Publishing, a job I've worked my entire career to achieve."

Thorton paused to gather his thoughts. "While I had more flexibility to travel to Spain with Isabella before the promotion, the board made it clear they expected me to be primarily based in the U.S. in my new position. Of course, Isabella and I tried to find a compromise. Still, nothing worked, and we began to argue more frequently. Neither of us was happy."

Kate softly asked, "Is that when you finally decided to divorce?"

Thornton leaned forward in his chair. "It all came to a head when Isabella's father passed away, and she was appointed CEO of her family business. Her entire family's financial stability was in her hands. Finally, she gave me an ultimatum—either I move to Spain, or she wanted a divorce."

Kate remained quiet.

"As painful as it was, we decided not to drag things out and agreed to the divorce. Isabella had her family's money and didn't need mine, and I didn't want anything that belonged to her family. Without children and with the financial aspects worked out early in the process, we navigated the divorce fairly quickly."

Thornton smiled. "Our lawyers laughed and said it was one of the quickest divorces they'd ever handled. And they got a big payday out of the quick settlement. We'd offered them a bonus to settle the divorce in record time, with the least amount of pain."

Quickly rising from his chair and walking closer to the fireplace, Thornton took a deep breath and released it before continuing. "And, sadly, that about sums up several decades of my life. You asked if I was okay. I can truthfully say I am now that it's all settled and behind me…except…" Thornton started to say something else, but he hesitated.

"Thornton, what is it? You know you can say anything you want to me."

Without thinking it through, Thornton blurted out what was on his mind. "I am over the divorce, but now and then, I feel slightly lonely, which surprises me. I'm in my early sixties, with retirement plans just a few years away, and I'm thinking about what's next. If you had asked me three years ago if I would ever miss having someone special in my life, I would have said you needed to see a therapist. However, as it turns out, having a special person in my life—maybe not another marriage—but someone to share special times, travel, and holidays, seems right to me. The type of person who would enrich my life. But only if it's the right person."

Thornton noticed Kate's cheeks flush. "Wow. Did I say that out loud?"

Kate and Thornton both suddenly began laughing out loud, releasing some tension from their bodies and minds. It seemed a good bout of laughter with a close friend was just what they needed.

Kate had tears in her eyes when they finally stopped. "Thank you for making me laugh. I needed that. I fully understand what you're saying. I've been widowed twice, and I can't imagine I'll ever marry again, but having someone special to enjoy time with might not be out of the question down the road."

Thornton was happy to hear Kate say she might be open to another relationship, but he knew not to push too hard at this point. She was still not back to her old self and needed to take things slowly.

A question popped into Thornton's mind: *Am I ready to take a step forward with Kate? What if things don't go well? Will I not only lose the opportunity of a special relationship but also lose one of my dearest friends?* He reminded himself, *Tread carefully. Very carefully.*

The two of them stayed in the library for several hours until Thornton had to return to his room for a conference call. Before he left, he shared several amusing stories about the mishaps in his condo building since the plumbing problems had begun.

At the same time, Cassidy happened to walk by the library and heard their laughter. She stopped short of the door when she heard her mother's distinct laugh and wondered who was in the room with her. It was good to hear her mother laughing. As Cassidy quietly continued past the doorway, she saw that Thornton was her companion, and they had pulled their chairs closer together. They seemed to be thoroughly enjoying themselves.

A broad smile spread across Cassidy's face. She thought to herself, *very interesting…*

CHAPTER FIVE

December 5ᵗʰ

The next morning in Room #210, dust was swirling everywhere.

Cassidy sneezed, talking to her friends who'd accompanied her to take a look at the reconstruction process. "The dust is worse than I thought. I'm glad we put up the plastic curtain in the hallway to block off the other rooms on this floor. Even so, we'll need to have the cleaning service do extra dusting and vacuuming every day until the renovations are done. I'd better call them now. We can't have everyone else impacted while this job is underway."

She stepped out of the room to make the call while her three friends sorted through boxes and arranged miscellaneous items into piles. Amanda, Trish, and Sarah had designated areas for "trash," "keep," and "donate". Fortunately, a truck was on the way from a local charity store to pick up the larger furniture pieces and several boxes of miscellaneous household items.

When Cassidy returned to the room, she paused in the doorway and laughed at the sight of her three friends, all covered with dust in their hair and on their clothes. Dust particles floated in the air, easily visible in the sunlight streaming through the large windows.

Walking over to one of the windows, Cassidy tried to open it, but she couldn't budge it since the windows in this room hadn't been opened for years.

"Can one of you help me open a couple of these windows? I know it's freezing outside, but maybe we can get a bit of this dust out of here."

Amanda, Trish, and Sarah walked over to the windows, each trying to open one of them. After much tugging and grunting, two of the windows finally opened.

"Oh. The air is too cold to leave the windows open for long. We just need a few minutes to air this place out." Amanda shivered, pulling her cardigan tighter around her.

The women returned to work. The chatter was minimal, as they had a goal to meet, and each of them was known for working hard and consistently hitting their targets.

Finally, Cassidy said, "I'm running downstairs to grab some water and make sure no one needs us, although our part-time desk clerk knows to call my cell should she need anything."

Cassidy checked with the clerk, and everything was fine. She grabbed four bottles of water from the dining room refrigerator and headed back up the stairs.

When Cassidy opened the door this time, the dust was significantly less, but the temperature in the room had dropped by at least ten degrees. "I think we should shut the windows. It's chilly in here, but I guess when we're busy and rushing around, we don't even notice it."

Cassidy walked to the back of the room, where an antique wardrobe was shoved into the far corner. She stopped to look at the beautiful carvings on the edges of the wardrobe. A door on the left side was the full height of the piece of furniture, and drawers were on the right. Her curiosity got the best of her, and she opened the door, but it was empty, as were all seven drawers. The mirror was cracked, and half of it was missing. Two of the drawers were also broken.

"It's a shame this wardrobe is in such bad shape. Otherwise, we might have been able to use it for storage. I'm glad someone is coming to move it for us. I bet it hasn't been moved in decades." Cassidy took a deep breath and gathered all her strength to move the wardrobe, but it was too heavy and wouldn't budge. "It weighs a ton. I'll leave it for the movers."

The women continued working for another hour when they heard the truck stop at the inn's service entrance. Cassidy went downstairs to show them the service elevator and then escorted them to Room #210.

There were four men, all of whom appeared to work out regularly due to their daily lifting of heavy furniture. They made six trips, and when they finished, the room was nearly empty except for the large wardrobe. The man who seemed to be the group's leader made one last trip back to the room. The name on his shirt was Bert.

"For a small donation, my crew will take all of these boxes marked trash to the dumpster I saw in the back of your building. We can get it done in one trip instead of you having to make twice as many. Will that work for you?"

Cassidy happily added a generous donation to the invoice and handed her credit card to the man. "We are thankful for your help. There's no way we could move these larger items to the service elevator by ourselves, especially the wardrobe."

The crew returned, removed all the boxes, and then came back with a large dolly to move the wardrobe. They tilted the piece of furniture, slid the dolly underneath it, tilted it back slightly, and then secured it with straps.

As the men began to roll the heavy piece of furniture away, it suddenly shifted on the dolly and banged against the wall. The workers quickly stabilized it, and once the piece was secure, they wheeled it to the service elevator.

"I'm so sorry about the small hole in your wall," Bert said. "Our insurance will cover it. Let me take some pictures for the claim." Bert walked over to the wall and snapped a few photos, but suddenly he stopped.

Bert ran his hand along the wall a few inches down from the small hole. "You might want to come over here and look at this. There seems to be a bump on the wall near the corner. Now that there's a hole in the wall, looking in, I can see some sort of small closet behind the drywall."

All four women hurried over to see what Bert was pointing at. Now that the wardrobe had been moved, it was clear there was a bump in the drywall.

Everyone looked at Cassidy, but Amanda spoke first. "Cassidy, do you want to see what's back there? It could be nothing, or it could be a hidden treasure."

Cassidy looked into the hole in the wall but couldn't see anything. "Since we are renovating this room, let's go ahead and tear out the drywall in that section of the wall."

Bert stepped forward. "If you're sure you want to tear out this section of the drywall, I'd be happy to do it for you. I have my hammer right here, and it should only take a couple of minutes."

"Yes," Cassidy said. "Tear it out." The women stepped back out of his way.

It took Bert two minutes to make several more holes in the wall and tear out the drywall, which was so old it crumbled in his hands. "Well, isn't this something? There's a small closet. Should I open it?"

The women moved closer to where Bert was working, and Cassidy eagerly said, "Yes, please open it."

Bert attempted to open the old-fashioned latch on the door, but it wouldn't budge. He then hit it with his hammer, and the latch sprang open. Bert opened the door and reached inside, pulling out a large bundle wrapped in a quilt. Several pieces of string were tied around the bundle. He carefully placed it on the floor. He reached back into the closet, shining his flashlight into its dark corners, but it was now empty.

Sarah was the first to speak. "Oh my, this quilt is an antique. It must be a hundred years old. I wonder what's bundled inside of it?"

"Let's find out." Cassidy joined Sarah and carefully started to pull back the edges of the old quilt. "There's more than one object inside. Sarah, can you help me untie these strings? Since I'm unsure what's inside, I want to be careful that we don't break anything."

The two women lowered themselves to their knees and untied the strings. Once they were undone, they pulled back the edges of the quilt, exposing its contents.

Everyone in the room gasped. Nestled inside the quilt was a beautifully hand-carved wooden nativity set, complete with Mary, Joseph, and Baby Jesus in a cradle, the stable, and the Three Wise Men.

Sarah examined the carved pieces, looking for markings or dates. "I've never seen anything so beautiful. The carving is exquisite. I'd say it's also from the early nineteen-hundreds and possibly German-made, based on the carvings on the bottom. With a bit of cleaning and some wood polish, it would be a stunning addition to your Christmas décor."

Sarah then gently lifted the quilt to examine it more closely. "While I love the nativity set, this quilt has captured my attention. Examining the material, thread, and pattern, I can see that it was well-quilted, most likely by a master quilter. The materials used appear to be high quality. I know a Quilt Historian in my artisans' community. I'm sure she can tell us more about it."

Cassidy and Sarah removed all of the nativity pieces and spread the quilt out. Sarah took several more minutes to examine the fabric. "Oh, look. The pattern resembles pine trees, which is the Maine State Tree, and the blocks are pieced together using red and green strips. The borders are also done in small blocks of red and green. This must have been a Christmas quilt."

"Maybe it belonged to the original owners of this building," Cassidy added. "I think it was initially built as a private residence for a well-to-do family from Boston, but I don't know anything else about them. Sarah, can you try to find out who this might have belonged to? I want to return the quilt and the nativity set to their rightful owners. I wonder why it was hidden in the wall."

"Of course, Cassidy," Sarah said. "I'll leave the nativity set here, but I'd like to take the quilt so we can better analyze the material and look for any signatures, dates, or initials. Quilters often added personal details in discreet spots on quilts they made during those times. Maybe we'll get lucky and identify the original owners."

Sarah took several pictures of the quilt and the nativity set on her cell phone.

"Trish and Sarah," Cassidy said, "I know you both need to get back to town to take care of business. Why don't you go ahead and leave now? We're almost finished. I appreciate all of your help."

Cassidy glanced over at Bert, who was helping clean up the drywall mess and putting it into large black bags. "I'll get this accident report filed with our insurance company," he said.

"No reason to do that, Bert," Cassidy replied. "We're renovating this room anyway, and if this little accident hadn't happened, we wouldn't have found the quilt and nativity set hiding in the walls. It's actually a blessing." Cassidy paused for a moment. "It's a Christmas mystery that only adds to the excitement of our special CLC plans, and I love a good mystery."

Bert picked up the trash bags and took them with him as he left. The two women finished sweeping the room and then carefully wrapped the quilt in a clean sheet Amanda had retrieved from the nearby linen closet. They individually wrapped the nativity pieces in old towels and placed them in a sturdy box.

Cassidy exhaled deeply. "I guess our work here is done. The contractor is scheduled to arrive tomorrow, and the room is ready for them. However, I'll need to explain the hole in the wall." She glanced at her watch. "It's time for a late lunch. I'm starving. Let's see what we can quickly put together in the kitchen. We also need to rescue Jack and Peter from watching our two little ones all morning. I hope Katie and Emma weren't too much trouble. I'm surprised we haven't heard a peep out of them. I'm not sure if that's a good thing or if we should be worried."

The women left the room and headed downstairs to Amanda and Peter's apartment, which had been added to the inn several years earlier. As Amanda opened the door, she quickly turned around and placed a finger in front of her lips, signaling to Cassidy they should be quiet. When she opened the door a little wider, they saw Cassidy and Jack's three-year-old daughter, Katie, fast asleep in her pack-n-play, while Amanda and Peter's two-year-old daughter, Emma, was asleep in her crib. Of course, Peter and Jack were also sleeping—one in a recliner and the other on the sofa.

Once they were safely away from the apartment, Amanda said, "I'm not sure who's babysitting who in that room, but let's hope they sleep long enough for us to grab lunch."

When they entered the kitchen, Amanda stopped when she saw a note on the kitchen counter and picked it up. "We thought you would be hungry and looking for something to eat, so we made you a tray of sandwiches and a large bowl of salad. The chicken salad is freshly made, and the bread is from the local bakery. Enjoy your lunch, love Peter and Jack."

Cassidy smiled. "How did we get so lucky to have such thoughtful husbands? Of course, we know Peter made the lunch since Jack can barely open a can of tuna." Cassidy walked to the refrigerator and started handing Amanda their lunch items.

While the women enjoyed their lunch and chatted about the morning's excitement, Cassidy reflected once again on how fortunate she was to have such an incredible group of friends, the inn, her mom joining them for the holidays—and now a big mystery to solve.

CHAPTER SIX

December 6th

It was holiday decorating day at Crystal Lake Inn. Cassidy always hired professionals to decorate the outside and inside of her beloved inn. She'd learned from experience the amount of lights and internal décor she desired would take her a month to complete, so hiring professionals had proven less stressful and much less messy. Instead of a month of confusion, it was limited to a few days. But, boy, oh boy, were those days full of people, equipment, crates, and chaos.

A large bucket truck stood in the front yard with workers in bright orange jackets hanging lights along the roof. On the ground, other workers were stringing lights around the bushes and along the walkway leading from the inn to the lake.

Inside, a crew wearing sweatshirts with the company's logo, Holidays Done Right, carried crates into the various rooms. Each public space, guest room, and suite would be decorated, and a small tree placed in each room.

Cassidy chose the small trees, which were pre-lit with twinkle lights and timers, yet not fully decorated. Guests could select their decorations from a supply waiting in the library or bring their own unique family ornaments with them.

Hooks for stockings would be placed on the large fireplace in the library for all the children, with space for others to be added if guests chose to do so.

By ten o'clock, Cassidy was already craving a cup of coffee. Walking into the dining room, she noticed her mother sitting at the small table near the large picture window, intently gazing outside. It seemed to Cassidy her mother was lost in thought.

"Good morning, Mother. How are you today? I didn't see you come down for breakfast earlier. Is everything okay?" Cassidy filled her coffee mug and sat down across from her mother.

Kate looked up at her daughter. "Good morning, dear. Of course, I'm fine. I opted to have my first cup of coffee in my room and took advantage of the delicious muffins Peter had delivered earlier this morning. I'm getting so spoiled staying here."

Kate gazed around the room. "It's starting to look a lot like Christmas around here. I can't wait until tonight to go outside and see the inn all lit up. I bet it will be gorgeous, as usual. Aren't those lights along the walkway new this year?"

Cassidy nodded. "I saw similar lights in town and thought how beautiful they would look here. The outside work is scheduled to be completed tomorrow, but the interior decorations, including the small trees in each room, won't be fully finished for a few days. I know from experience, though, they keep the mess to a minimum."

"As soon as I finish my coffee, I'm happy to jump in and help," Kate offered.

"Absolutely not," Cassidy said.

Kate wanted to be helpful. "Cassidy, I'd love to help decorate the library. I've already spoken to Wendy, the woman coordinating the overall decorating, and she said the tree in the library, which was placed there yesterday, would be available for decorating around noon today. Let me feel useful. I promise to follow the drawings Wendy put in each room, which show what needs to be done. You know I have excellent taste in decorating."

"Yes, you do have excellent taste, but you must promise not to climb on the ladder or lift any heavy boxes. Do you promise, Mother?"

Kate broke into a big smile. "Thank you, Cassidy. I promise to be a good girl. I'm eager to get started. By the way, did you see Thornton this morning? I want to say goodbye to him today, as he plans to take the early train back to the city tomorrow. The contractor called him late yesterday and said his condo will be ready tomorrow afternoon."

Cassidy shook her head no. "Jack told me Thornton had a series of conference calls and would be in his room most of the day. Before I forget to tell you, Jack extended the invitation to Thornton for him to return to the inn to spend Christmas with us, but he declined, saying he was looking forward to a quiet holiday this year."

Kate was disappointed to hear Thornton wouldn't be joining them, but she understood. On the other hand, it might be for the best after her reawakened feelings for him, which made her very nervous.

Setting her coffee mug down, Cassidy met her mother's gaze. "Mother, you look disappointed. Is there anything I should be aware of? The other day, I saw you and Thornton looking cozy, laughing in the library."

Trying to sound lighthearted, Kate replied. "What are you talking about? You're aware that Thornton and I are close friends. It was a gloomy day outside, and we enjoyed the fire and a good chat."

Smiling at her mother, Cassidy said, "Whatever it was, it was good to hear you laughing and see you smiling. You've only been here a week, and I think you're adjusting quite well. I'm delighted you agreed to stay with us. This holiday will be the best Christmas ever at Crystal Lake Inn."

Cassidy's phone buzzed in her pocket. "Excuse me, Mother, I need to take this call. I'll catch up with you later." With that, Cassidy walked back through the kitchen, leaving Kate to finish her coffee.

What were her feelings? Did she actually have a shift in her feelings for her old friend? *So many questions*, Kate thought, *and all without answers*. She decided to do something more constructive and headed for the library.

The crew had already started decorating the tree, but had stopped for their lunch break. Kate looked around to make sure Cassidy wasn't nearby. She didn't want to be coddled. She was fit and capable of climbing the ladder. The tree was already stunning. Standing just under fifteen feet tall, the live pine tree was full and smelled like the forest, but Kate noticed an empty spot about a third of the way down from the top, and she wanted to hang a few additional ornaments in that space.

Standing on the top step of the ladder, she filled in the bare spots. Since that worked out well, and she didn't even wobble while reaching over her head, she decided to add the beautiful, shiny, red iridescent ball to another spot. She climbed back down the ladder, found the ornament, and climbed back up.

Kate should have moved the ladder slightly to her left. She couldn't reach the spot she wanted to fill with the ornament. She leaned as far as she could, but couldn't reach it. Not to be defeated, she decided to climb back down the ladder and slide it to the left.

On her way back up the ladder, a sound behind her caught her attention. She was worried it might be Cassidy. Kate made the mistake of turning around to see who had entered the room. As she twisted her body around to look, she lost her footing.

Kate felt herself falling. She tried to grab the ladder with both hands but couldn't get a firm grip. Suddenly, all she felt was space and air. She braced herself for a hard fall to the floor.

In the split second before she hit solid ground, she felt a strong pair of arms catch her, but the force of her landing brought them both to the floor. Fortunately, her rescuer prevented her from a rough landing.

"Kate, are you okay?"

Looking down to see who was beneath her, Kate said in a breathless voice, "Thornton, oh no. Are you okay? Are you hurt?"

They both took a second to determine if anything was broken, and when they realized they were both unharmed, except maybe for their pride, they started to laugh.

Kate spoke first after catching her breath. "Thank you for saving me, but you put yourself in danger. I would have been fine. Let me get off you first, and then you can get up."

Rolling over onto the floor, Kate sat up and straightened her blouse. Everything seemed to be okay.

Thornton sat up, and nothing appeared to be broken.

"I bet we'll both be sore tomorrow, but thanks again for being my cushion so I didn't hit the floor too hard. Cassidy warned me not to get on the ladder. You know, it's your fault I fell. I was so worried it was Cassidy walking into the room that I got tense and turned around to see who was behind me, and that's when I lost my footing."

Slowly standing up, Thornton tucked in his shirt and ran his hand through his hair. "I saved your life, and you're going to blame me for your fall? I agree with Cassidy. There's an entire crew working to put up the decorations…so why were you on the ladder, anyway?"

"I saw a few empty branches, and then I noticed these beautiful red globe-like ornaments, and I couldn't help myself. Can we keep this little incident between the two of us?"

Thornton reached down to help Kate to her feet. As she stood up, she swayed slightly, and Thornton pulled her closer to ensure she was stable.

Kate looked up and saw Thornton intently gazing into her eyes. She felt the pull between them as Thornton leaned his head down. She was certain he was moving toward her lips.

And more importantly, Kate suddenly realized she wanted Thornton to kiss her, so she tilted her head slightly. As his lips lightly brushed against hers, she felt a tingle of electricity coursing through her body. The kiss was sweet, transporting her back decades to their first kiss in college, which had been equally sweet and innocent.

She craved more. Kate ran her hands around his neck, their bodies now molded together. Her body ignited. She was lost in the moment, oblivious to the world around them.

That's when they heard a loud thud outside the room. Kate jumped back, and Thornton dropped his arms.

Kate felt flustered. *What now?* She was slightly embarrassed. Smoothing down her clothes, she took another step back.

Thornton was the first to speak. "Kate, that was unexpected, but it was also wonderful. I've wanted to do that since we had dinner on our first evening here. I've always wondered if there was something between us. I guess I know the answer now."

Kate felt the heat on her cheeks and knew she was blushing. "Thornton, that was unexpected, and nice…but I'm not sure it's a good idea. If we tried and things didn't work out, we could ruin a forty-year friendship. Other relationships could be negatively impacted. You're also a big part of Jack and Cassidy's life."

Thornton tried to interrupt her, but Kate raised her hand to silence him. "Let me finish. We're both emotionally vulnerable right now. We need to think about this before we let it go too far. If I'm being honest, there may be something for us to explore, but we need to wait until after the holidays. You have me all twisted up inside. I need time to think. Too much has happened to both of us over the past few years, and we owe it to ourselves and the others around us to sort out our lives before taking any steps forward."

Thornton stepped toward Kate, but she quickly stepped back, left the room, and headed toward the stairs.

Once Kate entered her room, she walked to the window that overlooked the lake. The view was breathtaking, especially with the snow resting on the frozen water. She settled into the overstuffed chair and rested her elbows on the small table.

Kate could feel her heart still pounding with a mix of embarrassment and something else. *What was I thinking when I let Thornton kiss me? I guess I wasn't thinking at all.* The worst part was that she'd actually enjoyed the kiss and the connection between the two of them. The electricity was there. She hadn't felt that way in a long time.

Can I let my feelings override my good sense? Oh my, I feel like a teenager who just had her first romantic kiss. I need to rein in my emotions. It's a good thing Thornton is leaving tomorrow, or I might make a fool of myself.

CHAPTER SEVEN

December 7ᵗʰ

It was a sunny yet bitterly cold day in Lakeview, typical for this time of year. Kate still had shopping to do and arranged to catch a ride with Peter, who had mentioned the previous evening he was heading into town the next morning.

Since it was too cold to walk and Kate didn't want to take Cassidy away from her decorating, she was happy to ride with Peter.

As they drove the short distance into Lakeview, Peter and Kate discussed the inn's special holiday plans and the added excitement of Jennifer and her family arriving the next day.

"I'm looking forward to seeing Jennifer and Michael again," Peter said, turning to smile at Kate in the passenger seat. "Of course, I knew Jennifer before she got married, but they moved to Europe within a year of their marriage, so I don't know Michael as well, and now I can hardly believe their daughter, Addie, is six! The last time I saw her, she was only nine months old. I've seen pictures, of course. I think she looks a lot like you, Kate."

"Yes, everyone says she looks like me, which makes sense since Jennifer favors me also. I can't wait to hug them all, but I need to catch up on spoiling Addie, just like I do with little Katie."

"And you spoil my little Emma as well. The gifts you sent from New York City always brought excitement whenever the delivery truck arrived, and we saw a package addressed to Emma. The matching Christmas dresses and coats you gave to Katie and Emma earlier this week will look stunning in their Christmas pictures. They'll look like little angels."

"As soon as I saw those outfits, I knew I had to buy them," Kate said. "I tried to get a matching outfit for Addie, but they are sold out. Now, I need to find something special for her. By the way, I appreciate you driving me to town. You can drop me off at Crystal Lake Gifts. Trish said she had a few outfits I might like for Addie that she was putting aside for me. After that, I plan to stop at The Book Nook, the shoe store, and then grab coffee and a late lunch at The Perk. Don't worry about waiting for me. I'll get an Uber back to the inn."

Peter spotted an empty parking space in front of Trish's shop and pulled in. "Call my cell if you change your mind about a ride. I should be headed back in about an hour, but I can always find something to get into until you're ready to head back to the inn."

Kate turned to Peter with a smile. "Remember, no hovering. I'll enjoy my afternoon of exploring the shops on Main Street, grabbing something to eat, and then arranging for a rideshare back to the inn. I have the app on my phone. Thanks again for the ride."

Watching Peter drive away, Kate smiled to herself. She felt fortunate that so many people cared about her well-being. She appreciated their extra thoughtfulness, as long as they didn't take it too far.

Walking into Crystal Lake Gifts was an exciting experience. There was always new merchandise, and she enjoyed browsing through the Lakeview Artisans section, which featured a wide range of handmade items.

Several years earlier, Sarah Jennings Spencer had pulled together the local artisan community to form the Lakeview Artisans' Cooperative Enterprise, better known as LACE, which seemed fitting. When Trish added space for their handmade items in her shop, the artisans finally had a retail space to sell their wares. During the summer months, LACE also operated a community market a few miles outside of town in the Pineview Mountains.

Trish made a smart choice when she expanded her gift shop a few years ago, Kate mused. Her shop was now the largest retail store in town. The addition of the handmade section turned out to be an even bigger draw than expected.

Kate pulled the door open and heard the little bell ring. She loved that most of the shops in town used a similar little bell. As soon as she stepped inside, the aroma of fresh-baked cookies hit her nose, yet it quickly mixed with the deep, woody scent of pine trees. She thought it was an odd combination until she realized the enticing scents were coming from a display of handmade jar candles to the left of the door. The scents were so authentic they were easy to mistake for the real thing.

Trish was busy at the checkout counter, which gave Kate a moment to notice that Trish still looked stunning, especially with those big blue eyes and blond hair. It made Kate smile when she thought about seeing her ride through town on her little red Triumph motorcycle in warmer weather.

Walking over to the counter, Kate caught Trish's attention. "Hello, Kate. I'm so glad you stopped by today. I can't wait to show you the outfits I set aside for Addie. I have two beautiful holiday-colored dresses with matching coats that feature little fur collars. I think you'll find one you like, but if not, there's still time for me to order something with rush delivery that should arrive before Christmas. Let's take a look."

After reviewing the outfits, Kate chose one in a stunning dark green velvet. She also picked up several other gifts. Trish had one of the clerks wrap them in glittery paper with big bows.

Trish turned toward Kate. "Did I mention that my new clothing line, Lakeview Designs, is sponsoring a brand of unique Christmas-themed sweaters this year? This is our first time doing it, and I'm a little nervous. I'm hoping it goes well."

"You are so talented. Of course, it will be a big hit."

"We're donating five dollars to the local toy drive for every sweater we sell. There are twelve different designs. Sarah and the local artisans' group worked on them and made patterns. I shipped them to one of my clothing manufacturers in New York. I've probably overordered, but I'm hoping they take off, and we can help buy a toy for every needy child in the county. Would you like to see them?"

"What a fantastic idea." Kate was excited. "Yes, show me the way."

Returning to the checkout counter, Kate said, "Trish, thank you for showing me the sweaters. It was hard to choose the ones I wanted for Jennifer and Addie. I'm glad you shared the design Cassidy purchased for her and Katie. Now, all four of my girls will be models for Lakeview Designs. Can I also get these boxes wrapped, please?"

An hour after arriving at the shop, Kate was weighed down with three large shopping bags, which contained one of the outfits Trish had recommended for Addie, along with two sweaters. Kate had also purchased Cassidy a pair of exquisite ruby red earrings with gold trim that would look fantastic with the dress her daughter planned to wear on Christmas. Unable to resist, Kate also picked up a gorgeous handmade off-white shawl for Jennifer and a silk tie for Michael. Fortunately, she already had Jack's gift wrapped and waiting to go under the tree.

To help welcome Addie home, Kate purchased several small gifts, including activity books and a loom with yarn. With Sarah and Tom staying at the inn for the holidays due to Tom's accessibility challenges from his broken leg, Kate planned to ask Sarah to help Addie with the loom and yarn. Kate hoped Addie would create something handmade for her mom. Jennifer would be thrilled with the gift from her daughter.

Trish offered to hold onto Kate's shopping bags and take them back to the inn at the end of the day, but again, Kate felt the need to handle her own bags. She hugged Trish and turned to walk out of the store when suddenly, there was a commotion inside the front door.

At first glance, Kate had no idea who the stunning woman was, but she recognized high-end clothing and accessories when she saw them. The woman stood at least five-feet-eight-inches tall and had long, dark hair that reached well below her waist. Her shoes resembled Jimmy Choo's latest design, selling for well over two thousand dollars, certainly not the kind of footwear one typically wore in Maine in the winter.

Kate realized Trish was awestruck and didn't move for a second, but then she walked over to greet the new customer. "Hello, Ms. Armanti. I'm Trish Cavanaugh Williams, the shop's owner. We are thrilled to have you stop in. Is there something special I can help you with, or would you just like to browse?"

The woman finally removed her sunglasses and glanced at Trish. Getting a better look at the woman, Kate now knew who it was. *What was one of New York's most famous fashion bloggers doing in Lakeview?* Kate stood by and watched the conversation between her daughter's friend and the renowned fashionista play out.

"So, you're the woman behind Lakeview Designs!" Ms. Armanti held out her hand for Trish to shake. "My old friend, Amanda Blake—well, I guess her name is now Amanda Blake Cooper since she got married—anyway, Amanda posted photos of herself wearing some of your clothing line, and I like the classic, yet casual look. Not for myself, you understand, but my mother refuses to wear any high-end designer clothing I give her."

She seemed to pause more for attention, then to catch her breath. "When she saw Amanda's recent online post wearing one of your designs called the Twelve Days of Christmas Sweaters, she begged me to stop by on my way up the coast and pick some up for her. Since none of her friends in the city have them, she's eager to buy them as Christmas gifts for her friends."

Kate smiled to herself. Did Ms. Armanti compliment Trish, or refer to her clothing line as back-woodsy?

Ms. Armanti seemed flustered. "I guess that came out all wrong. It was meant as a compliment. My mother is extremely hard to please. Can you show me the holiday sweaters, please?"

Trish smiled and led the way to the sweaters, looking like she was floating.

Ms. Armanti examined the different designs and finally said, "I'll take six in women's small, four in medium, and two in large. Luckily, my mother told me the sizes she wanted before I left home. You can mix up the sweaters by size, but in the end, I only want one of each of the twelve unique designs."

Taking a glance around, with nothing else apparently catching her eye, Ms. Armanti said, "I think that will do it. Can you wrap each separately and write the size in small print in the right-hand corner on the tags? That way, my mother can decide who gets which one."

Trish nearly stammered out a response, she was so excited. "Yes, we can wrap them. I'll help the girls so it's done as quickly as possible. Feel free to look around or have a seat. There are comfortable chairs over by the fitting rooms." Trish turned quickly and walked away.

Ms. Armanti's assistant had been making online posts since they arrived. Word spread quickly along Main Street, and a crowd had gathered inside the gift shop. Ms. Armanti turned around and smiled at her admirers. Not surprisingly, Kate noticed that many of the young women were asking to have their pictures taken with Ms. Armanti. She agreed and offered to have her assistant take photos with each person's phone. She also asked several young women around her to turn on their video function.

"I'm here today at Crystal Lake Gifts, located at 300 Main Street in Lakeview, Maine. You should visit this cute little shop or check out their website. As you know, I'm all about supporting charities, and the owner, Trish Cavanaugh Williams, has a line of unique holiday sweaters called the Twelve Days of Christmas Sweaters. They're perfect for coordinating with your friends, and guess what? Trish is donating five dollars to the local toy drive for every sweater sold. To help out, I'm committing to making a cash donation to match hers."

Ms. Armanti slightly lowered her voice for the following words: "My lawyers make me say this, but I'll match up to the limit Trish put in her ad, so check the small print."

Continuing with her video, she chirped, "That's it for me today. My twelve sweaters are wrapped, and I'm ready to return to the big city. See you all soon. And, remember, Shop till you drop!" She finished by placing her hand on her lips, giving it a big kiss, and turning her palm around to the camera to show the outline of her lips, coated in bright red lipstick, on the palm of her hand.

"Cut! Okay, that's enough. Someone get me a paper towel to get this stuff off my hand, and I need a Perrie. I'm parched."

There was total silence as soon as Ms. Armanti and her entourage left the shop. To Kate, it felt as if a massive wave had entered the store, done its damage, and quickly gone back out to sea.

Trish finally gathered herself together. "WOW! That was amazing! Ms. Armanti is one of the biggest fashion bloggers in New York City. I was shocked when she walked in, or rather, waltzed in. If that video goes viral, it will be fantastic for sales."

Quickly, Trish's body language changed. "Oh my! Will I be able to keep up with the orders? I need to call my suppliers and Sarah immediately. Kate, thanks again for always supporting my shop. I can't wait to see those outfits on your granddaughters. Sorry, but I've got to get busy."

Kate noticed Trish's expression, a mix of excitement and a hint of fear. Interesting, she thought, but assumed Trish understood better than she did what a famous blog going viral would mean for her sales. *I guess it's a good thing.* But she didn't fully understand the potential impact.

Kate lugged her bags across the street to The Perk. By the time she had crossed Main Street, she already knew she should have accepted Trish's offer to hold her bags and take them back to the inn for her. Too late, she realized that her stubbornness was the cause of her arms feeling stretched and achy.

Before she entered the coffee shop, she could already smell the rich aroma of coffee mingling with cinnamon and the scent of freshly baked bread. She heard her stomach growl.

Walking inside, she headed toward the front counter. As soon as Amy, the owner of The Perk, saw Kate, she came out from behind the glass display case.

"Hello, Kate. It's so good to see you. Wow, you've been shopping and helping to boost Lakeview's economy. Let me take some of your bags and find you a seat. Then, I'll get your order." Amy lifted several bags off Kate's arm and pulled out a chair at the table near the front window.

Kate sat down and exhaled deeply. "Thank you so much, Amy. I love to shop, but my arms don't seem to share the same sentiment. There were a few items I wanted to buy before Jennifer and her family arrive tomorrow, but it looks like I might have gone a little overboard. I'm so excited to have them home."

"I heard that Jennifer and her family were finally returning from Europe. I haven't seen her since they left several years ago. I told Cassidy I'd love for us to have a girls' night out sometime soon." Amy pulled out her order pad.

"I could use a strong cup of coffee," Kate said. "What do you recommend for a late lunch?"

"We have freshly made chicken salad on ciabatta, a grilled tomato and pesto sandwich on focaccia, and classic tuna salad on soft white bread. You can complement any of those with a small side salad. Plus, there's still a variety of muffins available. What would you like besides the coffee? I remember you prefer it black. Is that right?"

"Yes, I still drink my coffee black. I can't believe you remember what your customers drink, even if they only come to the shop occasionally. I'll accept your offer of the grilled tomato and pesto on focaccia, accompanied by a side salad and light Italian dressing. It sounds perfect. I didn't realize I was so hungry until my stomach started growling."

"I'll bring your coffee out, and your lunch will be ready in a few minutes." Amy wrote down Kate's order and walked away.

Before Kate could pull her phone out of her purse to check for messages, Amy returned with a delicious-smelling cup of coffee.

"This coffee smells divine, and I need it after a morning of shopping," Kate smiled at Amy. "You're a lifesaver."

"One of the girls will bring out your lunch shortly."

Kate checked her phone and saw a message from Cassidy offering to come into town and pick her up when she was ready to return to the inn. With so many packages, letting Cassidy pick her up might be better, but Kate felt like she still needed to show her independence. She replied that she still had more errands to run and would get a ride-share later.

Kate's lunch arrived, and she eagerly dug in. Everything tasted delicious.

While eating, Kate enjoyed people-watching. She noticed a few acquaintances and a couple of women from the Lakeview Center for Performing Arts, which she had supported for years. They exchanged friendly remarks, mainly about the upcoming performance of The Nutcracker and their excitement about Karina Celeste coming to town.

After finishing every last bite of her sandwich and most of her salad, Kate pushed her plate aside and pulled her coffee closer. Seeing that she was done, Amy came over with a fresh cup of coffee and cleared away her dirty dishes. "Can I get you anything else?" Amy asked.

"The meal was delicious, Amy. It's wonderful to see your business grow every time I visit. I know how hard you've worked to make it a success. I'm so proud of you and all the local businesswomen. I'll sit here for a few minutes and finish my coffee. Thanks again for the great recommendations for lunch. I don't think I'll need dinner after this meal."

Amy walked away and paused at a few tables to refill coffee cups and check if anyone needed anything. It was late afternoon, and the café was less busy than when Kate had arrived. She scrolled through her phone, looking at a post made by Ms. Armanti. Kate was so absorbed in her activity that she didn't notice someone standing at the end of her table until she heard them clear their throat, indicating they wanted her attention.

Looking up, Kate was surprised to see Thornton. "What are you doing here? I thought you'd be in New York City by now. What happened?"

Thornton smiled. "I'd be happy to answer your questions, but first, let me order something to eat and drink. I'm starving." He walked over to the counter where Amy was standing. She took his order and said she'd bring it to him, but first, she poured his much-needed coffee.

Then Thornton joined Kate, having a seat at her table. "Okay, here's how my morning went. I got up very early to return the rental car and still catch the six o'clock train from Portland to Boston and then from Boston to New York. Everything was going as planned. While I was waiting for the connecting train in Boston, the contractor called with bad news."

Kate quickly inhaled. "What happened?"

"The job at my condo was completed and inspected late yesterday. Everything was fine, and the tenants involved in the repairs were informed they could return starting today. However, when the contractor arrived this morning to double-check everything, he discovered that one of the brand-new pipes had cracked. The condos on the top two floors, including my penthouse, appeared to have suffered the worst damage."

"Oh no," Kate said. "How bad is it?"

"While my condo isn't completely flooded, there is water damage in the kitchen and bathrooms, and the heating system is underwater. Everything will need to be redone. I'll have to be out of my condo longer now than I initially thought. The contractor estimated it would take four to six weeks."

Kate reached across the table and placed her hand on Thornton's. "I'm so sorry to hear this news, and I can't imagine the nightmare it's creating for you and others. Is the contractor doing anything for the tenants?"

"Yes, he's making arrangements for the impacted tenants to return to our condos a few hours later this week to pick up personal items and meet with our insurance adjusters. After that, we're not allowed back until the job is finished and inspected. It's unbelievable, especially for those with children. What will they do about Christmas? I feel bad for them."

Quickly downing several large gulps of coffee, Thornton explained. "Since I was closer to Lakeview than the city, I hopped on the next train headed back to Portland, and here I am looking for a place to stay until after the first of the year."

Kate suddenly realized her hand was on Thornton's. She slowly removed it, pretending she needed it to pick up her mug.

Smiling up at Kate, Thornton asked, "What do you think the odds are of me getting the same suite back at the inn? I only checked out a few hours ago. If not, I might have to return to Boston or the city to find a place to stay."

Kate quickly ran through her conversations with Cassidy about the plans at the inn. She thought Cassidy had mentioned leaving one room available for emergencies. She'd ask Cassidy to give it to Thornton. "Let me call Cassidy right now to see if your suite is still available."

Kate picked up her phone to call Cassidy, but was surprised to see her daughter was calling her instead. "Hello, Cassidy. I just picked up my phone to call you. What's up?"

Kate listened for a minute, and then a smile spread across her face. "Cassidy, that's wonderful."

It appeared that Thornton had texted Jack about the incident at his condo, and Jack had asked Cassidy if Thornton could extend his stay through the new year. She managed to work it out and called Thornton to confirm. The suite he just checked out of, #209, was left vacant on purpose in case of an emergency. This situation absolutely qualified as an emergency, but he didn't answer.

Cassidy responded, "Jack mentioned that Thornton was headed back to Lakeview and stopping in town to do some shopping. I thought you might see him there."

"There's no need to call Thornton. He's sitting here with me at The Perk. Kate handed her phone to Thornton. He listened briefly and said, "That's fantastic, Cassidy. I can't thank you enough. And no, the construction at the end of the hall hasn't bothered me at all. Thank you so much for finding room for me at the inn and inviting me to join the special events. It will feel more like Christmas to have a family to share the experience with, especially little ones."

Kate couldn't hear what Cassidy had said, but she heard Thornton laugh and reply, "I'm not worried about the children's noise level. It's nice to hear their laughter. I'll let you know if the construction or the children get too loud. Thanks again. You're a lifesaver."

Thornton returned the phone to Kate. "Cassidy, thanks for making room at the inn for Thornton. The Christmas story about not having room at the inn popped into my mind. I'm glad you worked it out."

Kate paused while Cassidy said something to her. "No, I still don't need you to pick me up. I'll call the ride-share in a few minutes." She glanced at Thornton who pointed to himself with one hand, and with the other, gave her thumbs up. "Oh, wait a second. Thornton just offered me a ride back to the inn. I hope that makes you feel better. He's grabbing something to eat, and I still have another errand to run. Don't expect us anytime soon. I'll see you later." Kate hung up and smiled. "Well…that was a whirlwind of a call. You are stuck with my loud group of family and friends for the holidays. I hope you know what you got yourself into, Thornton."

"Yes, I do. Bring it on. It will be fun. If I need some quiet time, Jack offered me the use of his home office. I think I'm covered. The best part is that we get to spend more time together if that's okay with you. I promise to take things slow, but I think you and I have some unfinished business."

Kate was taken by surprise at Thornton's statement. "Let's see how things go. No promises, my friend."

The couple sat at The Perk for another hour, made a few stops for Thornton to purchase items for his extended stay, and then headed back to the inn.

During the short drive back, Kate remained quiet, lost in thought. She felt a mix of emotions about Thornton staying at the inn and being so close to her every day. On one hand, she was nervous about rekindling the spark from earlier in the week. But, on the other hand, it felt wonderful to have a good friend who understood this phase of her life. A few sweet moments shared between them had already added to her holiday spirit. She just needed some time alone to think things through.

CHAPTER EIGHT

December 8th

Early that evening, it looked like a tornado had swept through several rooms of the inn. Suitcases, bags, shoes, coats, and toys were scattered all over the place. Fortunately, only two rooms were occupied by guests other than family and friends, and they were checking out on the eleventh.

Jennifer and her family had arrived around six o'clock. Once inside the inn, the noise level rose by a few decibels. There were hugs, tears, and shouts of joy.

Cassidy and Amanda ran behind the group, trying to keep a safe path from the lobby to the living room and dining room, so their guests wouldn't be in danger of tripping over items left in the natural pathway people used in the inn's common areas.

Peter, always thinking about the need to feed people, had prepared a meal in advance, including side dishes and desserts. He quickly retrieved them from the kitchen and arranged them in the dining room, where everyone gathered.

Jennifer walked over to where Kate was sitting and sat down. "Mother, I'm so happy to be home. It's been almost a year since I last saw you in person, and that was too long ago."

Kate smiled through her tears of joy. "Yes, I feel so blessed to have my family under one roof for the next few weeks. I don't know why I'm so emotional. I was worried a last-minute change would prevent you, Michael, and Addie from coming home. I know how things can change so quickly with Michael's job."

Hearing his name, Michael walked to where his wife and mother-in-law were sitting together and pulled up a nearby chair to join them.

Kate noticed a momentary flicker of concern on Jennifer's face. "Jennifer, is everything ok? You looked concerned for a moment."

Jennifer sighed. "Yes, Mother, everything is okay. There is just a slight bump in the road."

"Yes, I'm afraid I have to go to New York City for a few days," Michael said. "The trip wasn't originally planned until after the holidays, but I got word of the change right before our flight left England."

"You still seem a little tense, Jennifer. Is there something else bothering you?" Kate asked.

"Addie was upset when we told her about Michael's business trip. I'm worried she's feeling unsettled. We've been away for several years, and Addie is only six. At her age, she's probably forgotten a lot about Lakeview, the inn, and her family. I know I can't rush her, but we all need to watch over her and help her connect the dots. We shouldn't assume she remembers everyone or everything in Lakeview. Michael's leaving tomorrow won't help the situation."

Immediately, Kate looked across the room at her granddaughter, Addie. She had always held a special place in Kate's heart since she was her first grandchild, and she was named after Kate's mother, Adelaide Grace, but everyone called her Addie. She had the same big brown eyes as Kate and Jennifer, yet her hair was blond, more like Michael's.

"Mother," Jennifer continued, "since you've visited us many times and you and Addie do video calls frequently, I hope you can spend some one-on-one time with her. Cassidy told me that Dr. Foster and his family are checking in soon, and their daughter, Ellie, is about Addie's age. I hope that helps her feel less isolated."

Kate reached out and hugged her daughter. "I'm looking forward to spending lots of time with Addie. You and Michael are wonderful parents. You'll find the best ways to ensure Addie feels secure and loved. Having everyone here will help. Perhaps having Derrick, our own uniformed officer, might help Addie feel special and protected. That alone should give her a sense of safety."

"It's wonderful that Cassidy has several close friends. I'd forgotten that Trish and her husband Derrick were also staying with us. Yes, having the Chief of Police from Lakeview with us should make us all feel safer."

"Speaking of feeling safer, having our very own doctor at the inn is also a bonus. Although his specialty is neonatal, Doctor Foster is a physician. However, if the weather turns nasty, he'll most likely be called into work."

Jennifer added, "I don't know the Fosters. Now I'll have a chance to spend some time with them. If I may ask, what prompted Cassidy to include them in the invitation?"

"You mean besides having a soft heart? She decided to include them when Tom and Sarah decided to stay. Dr. and Leah Foster are wonderful people and have been a great addition to the community. Leah is Tom's sister. She was delighted when she heard her daughter would have a playmate. If the doctor is called to the hospital, Leah and the children could be alone for Christmas. Hopefully, we can fill the void and include them in everything we do. The CLC appears to have benefited several families."

Their conversation was interrupted by Peter, who turned to Jennifer. "I know it's been a hectic and stressful day for you, Michael, and Addie, as well as the nervous Nellies here at the inn, my wife included, who peeked out the windows every few minutes, waiting for you to arrive. I suggest we all grab some food, sit down, and enjoy a meal together."

"Here, here." Michael stood and looked at the buffet table. "I'm starving."

Everyone filled their plates and gathered around the large dining room table, which Amanda had thoughtfully decorated with a Christmas theme. Thanks to the creative centerpiece she crafted earlier that day, the room was filled with the subtle scent of pine trees. She collected fresh pine cones from the property, arranged them among short pine branches, and placed candles in the center.

The fine china was arranged on a Christmas-patterned tablecloth, and each place setting featured a printed index card detailing the special events Cassidy had planned for their CLC.

Kate looked around the table and said a special prayer, grateful to have her family together and to be surrounded by so many people she loved.

There was a lull in the conversation, so Cassidy asked, "Jennifer, we heard you had a few mishaps closing up your home and flying here. Would you care to share?"

Kate could tell that Jennifer was thinking about the question Cassidy had asked her, and Jennifer's face lit up when she quickly glanced over at her husband before replying. You could see the love in her eyes.

Jennifer and Michael experienced a whirlwind romance when they both landed jobs at the U.S. State Department in Washington. They were a perfect match in so many ways—both had similar physical features, except for hair color, but they also shared similar personalities—a bit more formal in the way they dressed, along with a tendency to be guarded in what they said, which was required in their jobs. Kate was happy for them, except when their jobs took them away from home. She wondered how long it would be before they were swept away again.

When Jennifer started talking, Kate was brought back to the discussion and away from her daydreaming.

"The funniest story," Jennifer started, "was when we couldn't find my passport. Everything had been going smoothly until I tried to gather all our travel documents into one folder, and suddenly, I couldn't find it. Since we traveled across Europe quite often, I was used to keeping it safe. We searched everywhere, but it was nowhere to be found, and there was no time to get a new one. We ended up unpacking about twenty boxes before we finally found it.

Peter asked, "Where was it?"

"You won't believe where we found it!" Jennifer exclaimed. "Addie was playing dress-up with one of her little friends, and I had given her a few of my old pocketbooks to use. When Addie saw Michael and me unpacking boxes, she got confused and thought we were unpacking to stay in England. She started to cry. When we asked her what was wrong, she wanted to know why we weren't coming to stay with Grandmother and Aunt Cassidy for Christmas, because that's where she told Santa to leave her gifts."

Jennifer paused to take a deep breath. "We explained that we were still going to the States, but my passport was missing, and that we needed to find it. She stopped crying, hesitated for a second, then jumped up and grabbed my old black travel bag from the basket she kept her make-believe outfits in."

Looking across the table at her daughter, Jennifer smiled and then added. "Addie ran over to me with the passport in her hand. She explained she didn't think it was my real passport because the photo didn't look like me. What could we do but laugh? I told Addie that most people's passport photos aren't a good likeness of their faces. And yes, this was my real passport, and I thanked her for finding it."

Those around the table laughed, then Jennifer added, "That was the first in a series of lost and found items, as we tried to fit too much into the maximum number of bags allowed on the plane, constantly removing items from our luggage that we urgently needed in our final days before leaving."

Michael shared a story about going through TSA when the agent asked Addie to place her doll in the bin on the conveyor belt. Addie told the agent her doll had a passport, and she gave it to him. It was a drawing that resembled her passport, featuring a round face with two eyes and a smiling mouth. She had written her doll's name at the top of the page.

Seeing the puzzled look on the agent's face, Michael shared he had then leaned down and explained to Addie that her doll would receive special treatment and a free ride on the conveyor belt. "She reluctantly placed her doll in the bin for the special ride. On the other side of the X-ray machine, the agent smiled and personally handed Addie her doll. He also thanked me for diffusing another potential crying child. There were several others in tears behind us in the long lines."

When Addie realized her father was telling a story about her, she spoke up, "Yes, my baby got a free ride. I told Daddy I wanted to ride on it the next time we were at the airport. It looked like fun."

Everyone laughed, and more stories were told.

Jennifer wrapped up the stories. "It's been a hectic few weeks. But now that we're finally home, I hope life settles down. We all need a break and look forward to a good old-fashioned Christmas in Lakeview and at the inn. There's nothing like a Crystal Lake Christmas."

As dinner came to an end, Thornton entered the room and greeted their new guests. He lingered just long enough to be polite, said his goodbyes, and then headed to his room.

Kate quietly got up from her chair and left the dining room. As Thornton reached the stairs, Kate approached him. "You could have stayed and enjoyed dessert or coffee with us. You didn't have to run off."

"I wasn't running off. I wanted to give your family time together. I thought it was best to head to my room."

Kate tilted her head slightly as she considered what she wanted to say. "We had a wonderful day yesterday, and then I ruined it by asking for time to sort through my feelings. I don't want it to become awkward between us. You've always been special to me, and you always will be. I'm just not sure I'm ready for anything more, but I'm keeping an open mind."

A smile spread across Thornton's face as he stepped closer to Kate. "Ahh… you're keeping an open mind, and I'm asking you to keep an open heart. But an open mind is a step in the right direction."

Thornton leaned over, gently kissed Kate's lips, and headed upstairs without looking back.

Kate stood at the bottom of the stairs, feeling a bit dazed. She couldn't believe Thornton had kissed her, especially in the lobby with her family just down the hall. What was he thinking?

Without Kate realizing it, Jennifer had left the dining room to see where Kate had gone. Jennifer turned the corner just in time to see Thornton lean over and kiss her mother.

Without being seen, she quietly turned around and headed back to the dining room, not saying a word to anyone.

Later that evening, after everyone else had fallen asleep or retired to their rooms, Kate, Cassidy, and Jennifer lingered in the library. A fire crackled in the hearth, and the only light came from the large Christmas tree in the corner. The fire, the lights, and the soft holiday music playing through the overhead speakers created a cocoon of gentle holiday ambiance.

Jennifer asked for a rundown of the special events at the inn and in Lakeview. Cassidy was eager to share, so she pulled out a flyer she had printed for the special CLC events. She explained that attending the events was optional, but she hoped everyone would try to join as many as possible as a family.

It seemed Cassidy hadn't changed during her absence. The flyer was extremely detailed, yet easy to follow. Cassidy was as over-prepared as anyone could be, and she was thrilled that they would be immersed back into life in Lakeview and at the inn.

After an hour, Kate couldn't suppress a yawn, so she kissed each of her daughters goodnight and went upstairs. As Cassidy stood up to sift through the ashes in the fireplace and extinguish the fire, she turned to say goodnight to her sister, but Jennifer stopped her.

"What's going on between Mother and Thornton?" Jennifer whispered.

Cassidy looked startled by the question. "What do you mean by something going on between Mother and Thornton?"

"When Thornton left the dining room to go upstairs, I noticed Mother also walked out. I wanted to see if she needed help with anything, so I went to find her. I got quite an eyeful when Thornton leaned over and kissed her."

"Did he kiss her on the lips? Did she return the kiss?" Cassidy was also whispering.

"I couldn't see everything because she had her back to me, and I didn't stick around to see what else happened. I rushed out of there before either of them noticed me."

"As far as I know, they're just good friends," Cassidy replied. "It's been nice having Thornton here. I don't know if anything romantic is going on between them, but I'm glad he's been able to pull her out of her depression. No. Wait. I wouldn't call it a depressed state, just a bit down and lonely, even with all of us around her. Since the two of them arrived on the same train and shared a ride from Portland to here, they've been spending time together, and I've seen a significant improvement in Mother's mood. She's been laughing more than I've heard her do in a long time. If something is going on, I'm all for it."

Jennifer remained quiet, clearly processing the information Cassidy had just shared. "If Thornton makes her happy, I suppose I'm okay with it. I hope she's emotionally prepared for it, though, after losing Duncan. Mother is one of the strongest women I know, but I'm not sure she can handle another big emotional letdown. For now, I'm in a wait-and-see mode, and if that means I need to do a little spying to get clarification, then I'm all for it. You and I always had a lot of fun spying on others when we were growing up. I remember Grams lecturing us that spying on people never led to anything good. We need to be careful she doesn't catch on. She wouldn't be pleased with us."

"Oh, so now I'm part of this little spy outfit?" Cassidy laughed. "Alright, I'm in…and mum's the word."

Jennifer leaned over to hug her sister. "I'm so glad we're home. Thanks for making this a holiday season for us to remember."

"Oh, I'm sure it will be!" Cassidy turned off the tree and the remaining lights, except those she always kept on for guests, and then headed to her room.

When Jennifer reached her room, she was careful not to wake her husband or daughter. She quickly got ready for bed but decided to sit by the window and gaze out at the lake, which reflected the bright moon. She'd missed seeing this view while they were away.

She replayed the scene from earlier when Thornton kissed her mother, and then when Cassidy shared her feelings about it. Jennifer wanted her mother to be happy, but she wasn't at a point where she could encourage her either.

She already had a long list of things to handle as she worked to get her family settled back into life in the US. She hadn't expected to deal with her mother's romantic journey too. To say life was interesting was an understatement.

CHAPTER NINE

December 9th

Downtown Lakeview resembled a scene from a Hallmark Christmas movie. Main Street sparkled with twinkling lights, fresh greenery, and the delightful aroma of cookies baking filled the air.

To enhance the ambiance, each store's front windows were beautifully decorated, some featuring animated characters and others showcasing eye-catching displays. The hardware store featured a train running along the large picture window, complete with smoke puffing from its engine. The Perk had an adorable display of Santa and his elves working in their toy shop, taking a coffee break with steam rising from their coffee mugs.

The town square, which was more of a circle than an actual square, served as the focal point of the Christmas Village. A dozen small wooden booths had been built, each adorned with twinkling lights and open fronts, making shopping easier.

Of course, the Lakeview Artisans group was showcased with several booths to display their handmade goods, including leather items, candles, locally sourced meats and cheeses, ciders, traditional wooden toys, quilts and placemats, roasted chestnuts, popcorn, and hot chocolate. Additionally, there were games for children and face painting. There was something for everyone.

It was a chilly day, with light snow flurries expected later in the afternoon. Everyone was bundled up warmly, many wearing boots, hats, and gloves. Anyone living in Maine understood the importance of dressing warmly and being prepared for snow on nearly any winter day.

Cassidy, Amanda, and Jennifer sat at The Perk, savoring cups of coffee and fresh muffins while watching people on the street. They'd left the inn after breakfast had been cleared away and had already done some shopping, including a stop at Crystal Lake Gifts. After their break, they planned to head to the Christmas Village.

Jennifer was happy to be home, and the warm atmosphere created by the beautiful decorations was quickly putting her in the holiday spirit. She found herself humming along to the Christmas songs coming from the overhead speakers when she saw her sister look her way and smile. She hadn't even realized she'd been humming out loud. The stress of the recent hectic move was starting to fade. But something still bothered her.

Jennifer took a deep breath and said, "Can we talk about the situation between Mother and Thornton? Cassidy, I know you said there wasn't anything going on, but that kiss lingered in my mind last night. Amanda, you've been around them this past week. Have you noticed anything?"

Amanda looked surprised by the question. "No, I haven't noticed anything. Although now that you mention it, Peter said Kate and Thornton were in the library for several hours the other day, and he brought them hot cocoa. But it was just a passing comment. Wait. Did you say you saw them kissing? That's interesting."

Cassidy appeared uneasy. "Jennifer, I don't think we should overreact to this just yet. Perhaps it was simply an innocent display of affection, nothing more. They're both single adults and have been good friends for decades. We should let it be. Can you imagine how embarrassed Mother would feel if you confronted her about it and the kiss turned out to be just a peck on the cheek? A form of endearment between two close friends? No way. Let's leave it alone for now."

"Okay, I agree," Jennifer said. "Let's finish our coffee and then head to the Christmas Village. I still need to buy several gifts. Sarah mentioned that one of the artisans has handmade shawls, and I was hoping to get one for Mother."

The women declined the offer of another cup of coffee, finished their muffins, collected their shopping bags, and headed toward the door.

Cassidy was the first in line to leave, but as she approached the door, she suddenly stopped, causing Jennifer and Amanda to bump into one another.

Amanda asked, "Cassidy, what's wrong? Why did you stop so quickly? There's no one in front of you."

Cassidy turned around and pushed Amanda and Jennifer away from the door. "Look outside. Mother and Thornton are out there."

The two women leaned around Cassidy to get a better view of the sidewalk. Kate and Thornton had stopped to talk to a woman with an adorable, light-brown Yorkshire Terrier. Cassidy knew the woman, Mrs. Perkins, who also served on the Board of Lakeview Hospital alongside Kate. The two chatted for a moment before Kate introduced Thornton to her.

Amanda spoke up. "Cassidy, what are we doing? Do you plan to hide in here all day? Let's walk out, say hello, and keep going to the Christmas Village."

"I wasn't aware Mother was coming into town. She declined my offer to join us. Let's wait a moment and see where they're headed," Cassidy replied.

Jennifer moved past Cassidy and headed back toward the door. "If they see us hiding, they'll think we're spying on them. This is ridiculous. What's wrong with you?"

The decision to go out the door or not was solved when Kate and Thornton said goodbye to the woman they'd been talking to and walked up the steps to The Perk. Thornton reached for the door and opened it for Kate, who walked inside with Thornton following close behind her.

Kate looked up in surprise when she saw her two daughters and their friend standing awkwardly just inside the door. "Well…hello, you three. Fancy meeting you here. I can see that you've already had success in your shopping spree. That's a lot of shopping bags. Where are you headed now?"

Cassidy was the first to respond. "Hello, Mother. Hello, Thornton. Yes, we've already shopped up and down Main

Street and stopped here to grab a mug of coffee and a muffin. Now, we're headed to the Christmas Village. Mother, I didn't think you were coming into town today. What are you two up to?"

Thornton had been quiet until now. "I asked Kate to help me find a few presents still on my list. She graciously agreed, so I offered to buy her a coffee and, hopefully, one of those delicious blueberry muffins she seems fond of. I hope they still have some left."

There was a moment of awkward silence. Finally, Jennifer spoke up, "Enjoy your coffee and muffins. We need to get moving. It looks a bit gray outside. I want to finish our shopping and get back to the inn before more snow falls. If I remember correctly, it gets dark around here before five o'clock this time of year. We'll see you back at the inn." With that, Jennifer nearly pushed Cassidy and Amanda out the door.

Once the door closed and the three women stood on the sidewalk, Jennifer turned to the others. "I told you something was happening between Mother and Thornton."

Cassidy turned to her sister. "Just because they're shopping together doesn't mean they're a couple. Didn't you ever go shopping with a close male friend?"

Jennifer smiled and replied, "Of course not. Did you?"

"Well…not that I can recall right now. But, I probably have. It doesn't prove anything."

Hearing Cassidy's response brought a smug smile to Jennifer's face, but then she noticed the sky getting darker by the minute. "We need to get moving. I want to get to the Christmas Village and back to the inn before dark. Let's hustle, ladies."

Earlier that morning, Kate was surprised when Thornton invited her to join him in town for some shopping. She'd already turned down an invitation to go into town with her daughters. She'd wanted them to have some bonding time without her tagging along.

Thornton mentioned he could use her help. He still had several gifts to buy and hoped to find everything he needed in town rather than heading back to Portland to the larger shopping malls. He also sweetened the deal by saying he would buy her coffee and a muffin of her choice at The Perk.

Kate agreed to go with Thornton, but she wondered whether it was a friendly invitation or more like a date. As she contemplated this question, she realized she wanted to go with him and was okay if it felt similar to a date. Either way, she felt comfortable joining Thornton. She further justified her decision by reminding herself she still had a few gifts to buy, so it made perfect sense for her to join him.

Running into her daughters and Amanda had been a bit uncomfortable. They'd acted a bit strangely. Kate got the distinct impression the women had been watching them from inside the coffee shop. *Probably not, or at least I hope they weren't.*

Once inside The Perk, Kate found a table away from the door, which was a bit warmer, while Thornton went to the counter to place their order.

Amy asked if she could help the next person in line. When Thornton approached, she had a big smile on her face. "You're becoming a regular here. We like that. What can I get for you?"

"Hi, I'm Thornton Reed. I'm staying at Crystal Lake Inn, and I'm a longtime family friend. I'm here with Kate. Do you have two of those delicious blueberry muffins? If so, could you warm them up a bit and add a pat of butter on top? We'd also like two black coffees."

"Ah, Mr. Reed. I believe you're also Jack's publisher. I'm a big fan of his spy novels and eagerly wait for each new release. We're happy to have you in town. And, yes, we made another batch of the muffins, and they're fresh out of the oven. That's Kate's favorite way to enjoy a blueberry muffin—warm and buttery." Amy told him the total for his order. He paid and told her to keep a generous tip. "You can take your seat, and I'll bring out your order as soon as I heat the muffins."

When Thornton sat down, Kate whispered, "Don't look now, but the town busybody just walked in. Mrs. Lester makes the rounds in town every few days to see what new gossip she can pick up. Sometimes, if she doesn't hear anything exciting, she embellishes old stories to make them more interesting. Hopefully, she'll grab her coffee and be on her way."

Amy approached their table carrying a tray, served them their coffee and muffins, asked if they needed anything else, and rushed back to the counter, where several people were waiting.

Kate and Thornton sat quietly, savoring the aromatic coffee and fresh muffins.

Thornton set down his coffee mug and turned to Kate. "Lakeview is such a lovely town. Most of the time when I'm here, I don't have time to fully enjoy everything it has to offer, and I don't get to appreciate it with such a wonderful companion. Kate, thank you for coming with me today. It's great to escape from work and enjoy each other's company. Plus, a fantastic cup of coffee and fresh muffins. I feel like I've hit the jackpot today."

Before Kate could respond, Mrs. Lester approached their table. She didn't wait for acknowledgment before saying, "Hello, stranger. I'm Mrs. Lester. Who are you?"

Thornton flashed his most engaging smile. "I'm Thornton Reed, a family friend of Kate's, and I'm staying at the inn. You must be the famous Mrs. Lester. It's good to meet you."

"Well, young man, you are the charmer." Mrs. Lester turned to Kate. "Hello, Katherine. I heard you were coming to stay at the inn, and I'm sure your family is happy to have you here, especially now that Jennifer and her family are back from Europe. Although it's a shame that her nice husband had to leave town immediately. I hope he'll be back before Christmas. Speaking of Christmas, have you visited the Christmas Village yet? They have a lot of beautiful items, and the homemade cookies are to die for. Everyone is buzzing about that famous ballerina coming to town. I'm not much for that, but I've heard she's very good at it. Sad, though, that she has to retire. She seems too young to give up on her career, but if your toes can no longer take it, it's time to step down. Get what I did there? Well, I won't take up any more of your time. I need to grab my coffee and head to the yarn shop, where I'm meeting a few friends from our knitting club."

Without waiting for a response from Kate or Thornton, Mrs. Lester turned and walked toward the counter.

"Phew…she's a whirlwind," Thornton remarked. "Did she even stop to take a breath?"

Kate let out a short chuckle. "I'm not sure Mrs. Lester needs air like everyone else. As you heard, she knows everything that's happening in town.. Be careful, or you might be her next victim."

After finishing their coffee and muffins, they headed to the Christmas Village. They strolled around the area, discovered several items to purchase, and returned to the stand that sold homemade jams and jellies. Peter had mentioned at breakfast that he asked the merchant to save him a case of his delicious strawberry jam. Thornton offered to pick it up since they were going that afternoon. Fortunately, Thornton found a parking spot close to the circle, so he didn't have far to carry the heavy box. Kate held all their bags in her arms.

When they reached their car, Thornton placed the case of jam in the trunk along with their shopping bags, then opened the passenger door for Kate. He winked at her as he closed the door.

As they drove out of town, Kate replayed their afternoon together. Thornton was always a gentleman, holding doors open and gently touching her back as he guided her along the bustling street and through the Christmas Village. He was entertaining, often laughing at things he found amusing, and he took the time to appreciate the effort that went into many of the handmade items. In short, he was the perfect companion.

He never pressured her for anything more. Well…the wink was cute. Maybe he had decided that being friends was the safest route for them. But she suddenly realized she would feel disappointed if that were the case. Wow…her emotions were swinging back and forth. It was all too confusing.

CHAPTER TEN

December 10th

The organizers of the Lakeview Christmas Village asked Peter if he would host a baking contest at the inn. This would be a new feature suggested by several local bakers in previous years. Peter agreed, and he and Amanda offered to organize the event.

Judging would take place in the afternoon, with contestants bringing their culinary entries to the inn that morning. Amanda set up several tables with linen tablecloths, fresh flowers, and various types of cake and dessert stands, creating a beautiful display. She also prepared coffee and tea for those attending the event.

Cassidy stood at the entrance to the dining room and gazed across the room. "Amanda, the dining room looks amazing. Thank you for putting so much effort into it. I'm amazed by the number of entries we received, especially since this is the first year of the contest. Even Sarah entered one of her family recipes. She found an old recipe box filled with index cards when she cleaned out her grandmother's house. The handwriting on some was so faded that she had difficulty reading all the ingredients. The Chocolate Fruit Cake brought back wonderful childhood memories for her, and she felt drawn to enter it in the contest."

Amanda walked across the room to look at Sarah's entry. "Why did she call it a Chocolate Fruit Cake? The slice she cut for the judges doesn't have any jellied fruit, only a few dried cranberries. Can it still be called a fruit cake if it doesn't have that horrible candied fruit in it?"

Cassidy smiled. "I asked Sarah about that earlier, and she said that was what her grandmother called it, and she wanted to be true to the original recipe. Look at how thick and rich that chocolate icing is. I don't think I've ever seen icing that looks at least an inch thick."

Walking over to the table to get a better look at Sarah's entry reminded Cassidy of something else her friend had mentioned. "Sarah shared that her grandmother made them a Chocolate Fruit Cake every year for Christmas and shipped it in a large metal cookie tin. She and her sisters used to fight over who would get the first piece."

Accidentally letting a small laugh escape her lips, Amanda added, "If you get too close to the Plum Cake, you can smell the rum. I think that one should be labeled 'for adults only.' The Chiffon Cake features red and green fondant that resembles the lights of a Christmas tree. I'd never have the patience to make any of these desserts. I'm glad we'll get to sample them after the judging is over."

Peter and two other judges were finishing up their tasting and went into the kitchen to discuss their scores privately. The bakers stood nervously behind their entries in the dining room, hoping to win the blue ribbon. The winner would also be featured in the "Around Town" section of the *Lakeview Gazette*.

As Peter and the other judges exited the kitchen, they walked to the front of the room, where Peter tapped a fork against a water glass to capture everyone's attention. "Judging was challenging. We had over twenty entries, and each one was delicious. We narrowed it down to the final three. If we could have the following bakers join us at the front of the room, please."

One of the other judges announced the names: "Mrs. Lester for her Plum Cake, Jody Cummings for her Applesauce Delight Bundt Cake, and Sarah Spencer for her Chocolate Fruit Cake."

A round of applause erupted as the three finalists moved to the front of the room.

Picking up the three ribbons, Peter made the final announcements. "As we said, all three entries were delicious, and judging was difficult. However, in the end, we awarded Third Place to Jody for her Applesauce Delight Bundt Cake. Second Place goes to Mrs. Lester for her Plum Cake, and First Place goes to Sarah Jennings Spencer for her decadent Chocolate Fruit Cake. I've never tasted such a moist cake with rich chocolate icing."

Peter handed each winner their ribbon, and there was another round of applause and calls of congratulations for the bakers.

"We're now going to cut all the cakes to share with you, along with coffee and tea set up at the back of the room. Feel free to stay and enjoy the desserts and catch up with your friends and neighbors. Additionally, we would like to mention that the entrance fees were all donated to the local animal shelter, and Cassidy, on behalf of Crystal Lake Inn, matched the funds. Thanks again for your generous donations and support of the baking contest and the animal shelter."

Mrs. Lester, never known for being a good sport, turned to Peter. "Hmmm... I thought my Rum Cake... my Plum Cake would win first place. I don't understand. That Chocolate Fruit Cake doesn't even have any fruit in it."

Without warning, Mrs. Lester snatched a fork from the nearby table, took a bite of the fruitcake from the plate in Peter's hand, and grimaced. "Too much chocolate, if you ask me. I'll stick with my Rum Cake... I mean, Plum Cake." Then, she grabbed her ribbon and stormed out of the room, mumbling all the while.

After Mrs. Lester was safely out of sight, Cassidy, Amanda, and Peter burst into laughter. They couldn't contain themselves. Once they had calmed down, they approached the other winners and congratulated them.

"Congratulations, Sarah. Your dessert was delicious. I bet each skinny slice has five hundred calories, but it's worth it," Amanda said. "It was fun to have the baking contest at the inn. I love the smell of freshly baked cakes. The aroma filled the inn all morning. Let's sponsor this event every year."

Cassidy started to laugh, and the others turned to see what had amused her. "Talking about how good it smells across the inn reminded me of a time when the inn didn't smell so great," Cassidy said. "Peter, do you remember the time when you went to help your mother after she had a fall? I tried to make fresh croissants, but the old oven went haywire and burned them to a crisp. The smoke filled the kitchen, and the smell spread through the inn before we could open the windows. Several guests ran downstairs, thinking the inn was on fire. Instead, it was just another example of my terrible cooking." Everyone joined in the fun and laughed as they recalled the situation.

Cassidy paused for a moment. "That reminds me. That's the day that a mysterious guest checked into the inn. He kept his DO NOT DISTURB sign on his door, and we thought he was some sinister spy or something. Turns out he was a mystery writer and the future love of my life."

Noticing that Jack had walked into the room, Cassidy added, "Speaking of the love of my life, here comes the man himself. Hello Jack and Thornton! You missed the baking contest."

Jack leaned over and hugged his wife. "But I see we still got here in time for some leftovers. Thornton, feel free to help yourself."

Thornton walked over to Cassidy. "Thanks again for coming to my rescue and finding a room for me. I appreciate the room and the invitation to join the CLC events. It'll be nice to be part of a traditional Christmas. It's been years since I've had that experience, and I'm looking forward to it."

"We're happy to have you. Let me get you some dessert." Cassidy and Thornton walked over to the table so he could choose what he wanted to eat.

Jack and Peter poured themselves some coffee and joined the others.

Thornton casually remarked, "I heard the long-range weather forecast earlier today. The weatherman mentioned the potential of a snowstorm near the holidays. So far, they're only saying it's happening as far north as Connecticut and southern Massachusetts, but it's worth keeping an eye on."

Jack glanced at his friend. "Thornton, remember you're in Maine now. Unless we're getting over a foot of snow, it's just flurries. I don't think it's anything we need to worry about."

Cassidy hadn't heard anything about a snowstorm yet. While she agreed with Jack regarding snowfall in Maine, she always kept any potential for a significant storm on her radar and planned accordingly, especially with an inn full of guests.

It reminded her to meet with Peter and review their grocery and supply list. She was known as the Queen of Preparedness and intended to keep her title.

Sarah stayed behind in the dining room after the others left to go to their rooms or run errands because she had an update for Cassidy on the quilt they'd found in the wall.

"Sarah, you didn't have to stay behind to help me clean the dining room, but I appreciate it." Cassidy picked up a tray of coffee cups and headed to the kitchen.

Following Cassidy, Sarah carried the last dirty dishes into the kitchen and loaded them into the commercial dishwasher. "I wanted to update you on the quilt research. I connected with a local quilt historian who holds a PhD in textiles and is a qualified quilt appraiser. She shared some details that I wanted to pass along to you."

Sarah went on to relay the details the historian had given her.

As Sarah suspected, the quilt was made between 1905 and 1910. While the Pine Tree design appeared fairly consistent, the individual trees were created from scraps, sewn together to form uniform-looking pine trees. The material was likely purchased in a larger city and sold by the bolt.

The fabric and threads were consistent with that timeframe, suggesting it was most likely pieced and quilted around the same time, by the same people. She identified two distinct stitching styles, indicating that two women worked on the quilt. Both women would have been master quilters. Their stitches were nearly perfect throughout the entire quilt.

During this period, quilting was considered a daytime activity because good lighting was necessary to see what had been completed and what hadn't. Candles and kerosene lamps were still common. Electric lights were being introduced, but they were available primarily in larger cities, and Lakeview was still considered a very rural small town at that time.

The historian, however, couldn't find any hidden names or marks to help her identify the original quilter or her family.

"That's all I know for now. There are still pieces of the mystery that need to be unraveled," Sarah said. "The historian offered us the chance to publish an article in *Quilters' Quarterly Magazine*. Since the magazine is published quarterly, we're lucky that the deadline for the upcoming issue is tomorrow. We have time today to write a fifty-word piece for the section called LOST & FOUND. I took the liberty of drafting something. I'm not committed to the wording."

Sarah handed Cassidy a piece of paper with the proposed article on it.

Cassidy read the short article aloud: "FOUND: Antique quilt. Master Quilter's quality craftsmanship. Approximately one hundred years old. Discovered hidden behind a wall at Crystal Lake Inn, Lakeview, Maine. The inn's owner seeks to return the quilt to its rightful owners. The pattern features Pine Tree squares. Please contact the email below for more information." She included the inn's email at the end of the article.

Sarah added, "It took some word-smithing to get down to fifty words or less. You'll notice I didn't include any details about the scalloped edges or their color. Only the rightful owners would know the exact color scheme. Any changes?"

Not giving Cassidy time to respond, she added, "Oh, and I didn't include the picture, but if someone contacts us with the correct details, we can email them the picture so they can confirm it belongs to their family."

Cassidy replied, "The article is perfect as is. Thanks for including the inn's email instead of my personal one.

While I hope we only receive honest inquiries, you know there will also be some spam or scammers. Still, I'm hopeful we can find the owner. If we can't, I'm happy to place the quilt in a sealed display box and set it in the living room. It's so beautiful, and too precious to hide away again. I can't imagine dedicating so much time to creating a family keepsake, only to have it lost for decades. Fingers crossed, we find the owner."

CHAPTER ELEVEN

December 11th

Christmas was just two weeks away, and it was the final day for regular guests to check out of the inn.

Once breakfast service ended, Cassidy asked Amanda to join her at the front desk to help expedite the checkout process and offer each guest a special holiday treat.

Peter had made a selection of holiday cookies and wrapped them in decorative cellophane with red ribbons. Cassidy thought it would be a special way to send off their guests, expressing her appreciation for their patronage, especially from repeat visitors.

Cassidy put on her brightest smile. "Good Morning, Mr. and Mrs. Connelly. We're always so happy to have you stay with us. You and your family have become regular guests, and we appreciate it. Are you headed home for the holidays?"

Mrs. Connelly replied, "This is the first year we aren't celebrating Christmas at home. Our son has a new house and a new baby daughter. He invited the entire family to enjoy the holidays with them. At first, I was a bit sad that we wouldn't have Christmas at our family home, but then, I realized it was time to pass the baton."

Amanda looked at the number of gift bags next to Mrs. Connelly's feet. "It looks like you did some shopping while you were in town. I'm sure the local merchants appreciate it."

Mr. Connelly remarked, "I think she bought out the entire baby section of Crystal Lake Gifts."

Mrs. Connelly reached down and picked up one of the bags. "Look at this gorgeous Christmas dress for our newest granddaughter. Your friend Trish pointed it out to me, and I couldn't resist. Of course, I had to purchase a couple of the special Lakeview Christmas Sweaters. I love that shop, and Trish is always very helpful with suggestions. She's learned my taste, and I can't resist the handmade, one-of-a-kind items."

Amanda assisted the Connellys in carrying their luggage and packages to their car, waving to them as they drove away.

As Amanda returned to the front desk, Cassidy commented, "That was the last checkout. Now it's time to get to work and finish the decorating."

"I don't know what's left to do," Amanda said. "The firm you hired was here several days, and the inn looks fantastic. What else do we have to do?"

Cassidy walked out from behind the desk and linked her arm with her friend's. "Roll up your sleeves, and let's get to work. I have a few surprises and some gorgeous handmade decorations I want to add to the trees and dining room. I also bought adorable gift baskets with festively wrapped snacks for each guest room. I can't wait to see the finished inn. It's going to be a sensory overload."

Four hours later, Cassidy and Amanda finally finished their decorating spree. They walked through the inn, guest rooms, and common areas, both marveling at what they had accomplished.

The massive tree in the living room was breathtaking. Sarah had donated several hand-blown ornaments for it. The glass caught the light from the bulbs already on the tree and reflected shimmering patterns around the room.

The nativity set they found in Room #210 was arranged near the Christmas tree, with flickering candles casting a soft, off-white glow over the scene. The statuette of baby Jesus was front and center in his cradle.

Christmas music played from hidden speakers throughout the inn's common areas, and the speakers could also be activated in the guest rooms. A hot cocoa station was set up in the dining room, with reindeer-shaped bowls filled with whipped cream, chocolate shavings, and mini marshmallows.

Extra throws and quilts were added to the living room, creating a cozy atmosphere. A large supply of firewood had been delivered earlier in the week, and a stack sat beside the fireplace. An antique train set ran around a circular track under the tree, with the engine emitting white plumes of smoke. Holiday-themed games and puzzles for both children and adults were arranged on tables and shelves, ready for friendly competition or quiet enjoyment. The usual china used in the dining room was replaced with a large set of Christmas Spode, a gift from Kate several years earlier. Kate had found the set at an antique sale at a former Vanderbilt estate in the Hudson Valley, and she knew it would be perfect for the inn.

Each guest room featured a small, pre-lit Christmas tree accompanied by a basket of ornaments, inviting guests to decorate. And finally, the entire inn smelled like a bakery. Peter was in a baking frenzy, preparing every imaginable holiday dessert and cookie.

Amanda told her friend, "It's amazing! The entire inn resembles something out of a Hallmark movie. It's never been more festive. This is your best decorating yet."

"Thanks for your help. Now we can relax and enjoy it," Cassidy replied.

The two women linked arms again and headed to the kitchen to grab a late lunch and some fresh-baked cookies.

Cassidy turned around one last time before entering the kitchen and looked across the lobby and living room. It required a lot of work and expense, but the inn looked exactly as she had envisioned. She could hardly wait for her family and friends to see it. Christmas magic had arrived at Crystal Lake Inn.

Cassidy was in her office finishing some paperwork when she heard the bell at the front desk ringing repeatedly. She immediately jumped up from her chair and hurried to the front desk, fearing something was terribly wrong.

Arriving at the front desk, out of breath with her heart pounding, Cassidy couldn't believe what she saw. In the lobby was a six-foot-tall stuffed Santa Claus, complete with a red suit, shiny black boots, and a long white beard. The stuffed Santa almost looked real. *Real... what was she saying?* It must be the shock of what she was looking at in her lobby. But, where did it come from? And she was fairly certain the stuffed Santa hadn't been the one ringing the bell. Walking around the desk to get a better look, Cassidy was confused when no one was in sight. In a loud voice, Cassidy said, "Okay, you've had your fun and almost scared me to death. Whoever put this oversized stuffed thing in my lobby needs to come out now."

But no one came forward. Cassidy was still trying to figure out where the Santa had come from when she heard the front door open. Turning around, she saw that Jack was returning to the inn from running errands, and their daughter, Katie, was with him. When Katie saw Santa, she burst into tears and ran to her mother.

"Jack, if you thought this would be funny, it backfired on you." Cassidy tried to hold her anger at her husband at bay. "Katie is only three years old, and she barely remembers seeing Santa at the mall last year. And, if you recall, she was afraid of him. This is not the way to help her get over her fear of him."

Jack looked confused. "Cassidy, I don't know anything about this rather scary figure. Who left it here?"

Cassidy picked up her daughter and walked down the hall to help Katie calm down.

Jack followed them. Once Katie calmed down, he said, "You really don't know how this thing got into our inn?"

"No, I don't. Someone kept ringing the bell on the counter in the lobby. I thought something was wrong and ran from my office to the lobby, but by then, no one was there. We have other small children staying at the inn. I'm worried the sheer size of Santa will scare them. What do we do now?"

Jack left the room and returned to the lobby to search for clues. Walking behind the Santa, he discovered a large envelope taped to the back. He opened the letter and burst out laughing.

"Cassidy, wait till you hear this," Jack read her the letter. "Jack, Cassidy, and Family, I hope you enjoy the life-size Santa. We ordered it for our annual display at our department store in Portland, but when it arrived, we realized the manufacturer had misunderstood our instructions. We had requested a small supply of six-inch stuffed Santas. Instead, they sent us six, six-foot Santas. We remembered that one of your early novels featured a mystery involving a large stuffed animal, and you knew exactly how to solve that problem. So, we thought, who better to send one of the Santas to than you? We hope you can put him to good use. Happy Holidays, Sam Morrison, CEO, Morrison's Department Stores."

Seeing that Katie had cried herself to sleep, Cassidy whispered, "Oh my. While I appreciate the gesture, I think Santa has to go. What can we do with it? Taking a page from the novel Sam mentioned won't work in this case."

Walking over to his wife to take the sleeping child from her, Jack stifled a laugh. "I think you're right. I can't imagine that NASA needs a fifty-pound Santa for their next shuttle mission. But I do have an idea. Let me put Katie to bed, turn on the baby monitor, and make a few calls."

Cassidy returned to the lobby to look at the giant Santa again. She hoped her husband could find a solution to their problem because, as much as she loved a good stuffed Santa, this one was starting to creep her out.

Before Jack could return, Peter and Amanda came down the hall from the Kitchen. They stopped mid-sentence when they saw Santa.

"Before you say anything, let me speak. No. I'm not sure why there's a six-foot-tall Santa in our lobby. Yes, I do know who sent it. It's easier if you read his note." Cassidy handed the note to Peter and Amanda.

"You're kidding me," Amanda said. "What do you think we'll do with this monstrosity?"

Thankfully, Jack came back, so Cassidy didn't have to reply.

"Our Santa has a new home. The captain of the local fire department would love to take him off our hands. He's the perfect size to sit on top of the long ladder they use in the Christmas Parade. A few years ago, their insurance company started prohibiting them from having one of their firefighters sit on top of the extended ladder due to safety concerns. With this guy on the ladder, they can securely strap him in and fully extend the ladder. The crowd will love it. They'll be here in about an hour to give Santa a VIP ride to the station. Problem solved."

As Cassidy turned to hug her husband, Derrick and Trish walked into the lobby. The interrupted conversation, and confused looks started all over again. As far as Cassidy was concerned, Santa leaving in an hour was sixty minutes too long. One of these days, she needed to write a book about being an innkeeper. On the other hand, people wouldn't believe half the stories she could tell. She'd better leave writing to her very capable husband.

CHAPTER TWELVE

December 12th

The Christmas Village offered special events for children, including face painting, balloon art, and the opportunity to visit Santa and take a photo with him. Cassidy, Amanda, Jennifer, and most of the family had gone to the Christmas Village to enjoy a fun morning with the little ones.

Thornton had been busy all morning in his room, attending meetings and making phone calls. He decided it was time for a break, so he strolled downstairs to get a fresh cup of coffee.

The inn was quiet. He remembered Cassidy mentioning something about taking the children to town, so he assumed he was alone.

After refilling his coffee mug, he walked past the door to the living room. He was surprised to see Kate sitting by the fire with a beautiful quilt wrapped around her legs. She looked sad, and he was unsure whether to interrupt her thoughts or leave her alone.

Kate must have heard him approaching the door. She quickly grabbed a tissue and dabbed at her cheeks. She gave him a small smile to greet him, but it didn't reach her eyes—clearly, the smile was forced.

Thornton hovered in the doorway for a moment, trying to decide his next move, but Kate decided for him. "Hello, Thornton. Please come in and sit down. I see you have a fresh cup of coffee, and I just made myself a cup of cocoa."

When Thornton didn't join her right away, Kate said, "I believe we're the only two people here right now, since everyone else is in town taking the children to special events. They should be back this afternoon. There's still a small fire burning in the fireplace. Join me."

Thornton walked over to the fireplace, grabbed two more logs, and added them to the fire. They ignited quickly, and the larger blaze warmed the area.

"If you're sure I'm not interrupting your quiet time, I'd like to join you and find out why you look so sad. Are those tears on your cheeks, Kate? What's wrong?"

Kate used her tissue again to dry her tears. She hesitated for a moment to get her emotions under control. "I was walking down memory lane, remembering trips Duncan and I made to Germany a decade ago to enjoy the various Christmas Villages."

Turning her head toward the fireplace, Kate seemed lost in thought, but then she continued. "I was thinking about the upcoming performance of The Nutcracker. It reminded me of the shows we saw at the Semperoper Ballet in Dresden, Germany. That's a historic theater, and its architecture is stunning. It was originally built in 1841 and reconstructed in 1878 after a fire. During the final months of World War II, parts of the building were destroyed again. The shell remained standing until forty years later, when it was fully restored. The Semperoper has hosted some of the world's greatest ballet stars and theatrical performances."

When tears returned to Kate's eyes, Thornton grabbed a tissue. He moved to sit next to her on the sofa, and without thinking, he dabbed at the new moisture on her cheeks. He wasn't prepared for Kate to break down. She was a remarkably resilient woman who had seemed to stay strong despite Duncan's death.

Feeling an overwhelming urge to protect Kate, Thornton pulled her closer, and she leaned against his light blue shirt. Her tears left small, circular marks on the fabric. He wrapped his arms around her and let her cry. Eventually, it seemed she had cried all her tears out.

As Thornton looked intently at her, he couldn't hide what he was feeling. He noticed that Kate seemed momentarily surprised by the emotion on his face. She quickly pulled back, but not before he caught a brief glimpse of a similar emotion in her eyes.

Kate quickly moved away from Thornton. "I'm sorry for my outburst."

They both remained silent, unsure of what they felt or whether they should acknowledge it.

Thornton's feelings for Kate, from decades ago, resurfaced.

Looking intently at her, he saw the question in her eyes but was almost afraid to speak, fearing it might break the spell that seemed to have fallen over them. He decided to leave it to Kate to make the next move.

In a whisper, Kate said, "My body is urging me to lean toward you, but my mind is screaming for me to stop. I don't want to jeopardize a four-decade friendship by making the wrong decision, but my heart tells me something different."

Thornton reached out, placed his hand on her arm, and gently pulled her to her feet. Kate shivered slightly. Her body arched toward him. He waited for her to make the next move.

Thornton noticed Kate's expression quickly change from confusion to a smoldering gaze. He moved closer and wrapped his arms tighter around her.

Kate once again felt the warmth of his body and the gentle brush of his breath on her cheek. She slightly parted her lips.

That was all the invitation Thornton needed. The kiss that had begun softly and sweetly quickly became more passionate. He pressed his lips against hers to part them further and explored deeper, connecting with Kate on a more sensual level. She wrapped her arms around his neck and leaned in closer to him.

They were lost in each other and in the moment.

Thornton was stunned when he thought he heard bells ringing. Wow! That was a first for him. When he heard the bells again, he realized the sound was the jingling from the inn's front door.

At that moment, Kate realized someone was coming through the front door. Panicking, she pulled back.

They quickly sat down, with Kate on the sofa and Thornton in one of the chairs near the fireplace. He noticed they were both breathing fast, and he could see a light blush moving up Kate's cheeks. He wondered, *Am I also blushing? Heck, I hope not.*

Taking several deep breaths, they both tried to appear as if nothing extraordinary had just happened. However, to Thornton, the world had changed in the past few minutes, and he planned to continue exploring where their emotions would lead them.

CHAPTER THIRTEEN

December 13th

The Nutcracker performance was breathtaking, and the audience showed their appreciation with thunderous applause. The standing ovation and calls for an encore lasted several minutes. Even though the curtains had closed at the end of the performance, the enthusiastic applause from the audience prompted them to reopen. Karina Celeste returned to the center stage, where she received a large bouquet of red roses.

The stage manager brought out a microphone on a stand and positioned it in front of the ballerina.

Karina Celeste gestured for the audience to quiet down. "Thank you so much for that wonderful acknowledgment of our performance. The students from the local dance studio were fantastic and deserve another round of applause." The audience complied, and the applause erupted once again.

More flowers were brought onto the stage and placed in front of the row of student dancers.

"As you may know, this is my last performance. I've been asked why I chose to have my final performance in

Lakeview instead of New York. It's simple. This is where my love of ballet began. My family spent several summers in Lakeview when I was young, and during one of those summers, I joined the local dance troupe. My passion for ballet was born here, on this stage, so it feels right to end my career here."

Trying to keep her emotions in check, she took a deep breath before continuing. "Thank you once again for the wonderful send-off into the next phase of my life. I will always hold a special place in my heart for Lakeview and ballet, but it's time to move beyond dance and see where my heart leads me. I will be forever grateful for this meaningful send-off."

The curtains closed again, but the applause continued. Finally, the audience began to file out of the theater. Kate had been instructed to keep her group seated, and an usher would come to escort them backstage. Her grandchildren were so excited that it was hard to keep them seated.

Before the usher arrived, Kate took a moment to remind the children to be on their best behavior when they went backstage. She instructed them to address the Prima Ballerina as Madam Karina Celeste and be sure to say how much they enjoyed the performance.

Addie tugged on Kate's arm. "Addie, do you have a question, dear?"

"Yes, grandmother. Yesterday, I heard you call Madam just by her first name. Should I remind you how to address a Prima Ballerina? Maybe you forgot."

Kate smiled down at her granddaughter. "Thank you for the reminder. You're correct. I'll make sure to address her properly." Kate had forgotten that children heard everything you said, even when you didn't realize it. Since she and Karina were friends outside of the theatre, she did use the less formal name. But she needed to remember that little ones were listening. Not being around her grandchildren every day, she'd forgotten. She briefly wondered what else they might have picked up on.

A few minutes later, an usher approached Kate's seat and led her and her family backstage. It was somewhat chaotic, but the usher skillfully guided Kate's group around stagehands, performers, and photographers, eventually reaching the door of Karina Celeste's dressing room.

A group of fans was already inside the small room, so the usher hurried them out. When Karina Celeste saw Kate, she rushed over and hugged her. "Thank you so much for coming today and making arrangements for me to stay at your daughter's wonderful inn. It gave me a chance to relax and mentally prepare for the first performance and today's rather emotional last performance."

Cassidy spoke up, "We are happy to have you at the inn."

Kate introduced the members of her group. Dr. Foster and his wife, Leah, joined them, and they presented a small bouquet of flowers to their daughter, Ellie. At eight years old, Ellie already had several years of experience in ballet but wasn't yet old enough to progress to en pointe. Ellie hadn't talked about anything other than meeting Karina Celeste during their rehearsals. Clearly, the young dancer was star-struck.

Karina Celeste leaned down and kissed Ellie on her right cheek, then on her left. She took a rose from her own large flower arrangement and tucked it into Ellie's hair. Looking up, she directed her comments to Dr. and Mrs. Foster. "Your daughter, Ellie, is talented, and I'm sure she will continue to perform on stage both in Lakeview and possibly even in New York."

Turning to Kate, Karina Celeste said, "It's clear that this young woman, whom I believe you introduced as your granddaughter Addie, is also a dancer. Her straight posture reflects that of a natural-born ballerina."

Addie was also star-struck and didn't respond, so Kate leaned down and whispered into her ear that it was impolite not to reply.

"Yes, Madam Karina Celeste. I'm a dancer and ballerina. We've lived in several European countries, and I've performed in many shows, but I've never met anyone as famous as you. Thank you for your kind words."

Karina Celeste asked, "What was the most recent performance you did?"

Addie didn't hesitate to respond this time. "It was Swan Lake. I was one of the swans, and our teacher played the role of the princess. A boy from the older class was the prince, and it took my breath away when he picked her up and swung her around. I want to be a prima ballerina just like you."

Karina smiled and replied, "Kate, you should bring these beautiful young women to New York and visit my new dance studio, which will open in a few months. I'd be thrilled to show you around the big stage and introduce you to some young women who are already training to become prima ballerinas. I believe you'll love the experience."

Kate profusely thanked Karina Celeste for the private audience and her breathtaking performance. As she leaned forward to hug the ballerina, Kate whispered, "I hope we can get together before you leave. I have something I'd like to discuss with you. Will tomorrow work?"

Karina Celeste appeared surprised but replied, "Yes, I'd like that. I'll see you tomorrow."

The group left the theater, got into their cars, and drove a short distance to Attilio's, a popular restaurant on the outskirts of town. Luckily, Kate had made a reservation months in advance. The restaurant was crowded, and the line at the hostess stand was long, but Kate's group was seated quickly.

The aroma was delightful, and the options featured homemade pasta, locally sourced ingredients, and an elegant dessert cart, with options like tiramisu and cannoli. Fortunately, the children's menu included chicken nuggets and mac and cheese. Although not very Italian, the parents appreciated the owner's awareness of foods their kids would enjoy, which allowed the adults to savor the featured Italian specialties.

Kate glanced around her table, feeling grateful for the moment. She had just enjoyed a stunning ballet performance, had a private backstage meeting with the renowned prima ballerina, and was now sharing dinner with the most important people in her life...including Thornton, who sat by her side and stealthily held her hand under the table.

As the meal progressed, there was comfortable banter among the siblings, spouses, and friends. The conversations allowed Kate to occasionally steal a quick glance at Thornton, and each time she did, he gently squeezed her hand. Though small, the gesture sent a warm feeling up her arm. She hoped she wasn't blushing, yet again.

Catching a knowing look between her daughters, she worried they were making more out of the situation than they should, so she removed her hand from Thornton's, pretending to help one of the children with their napkin. But, as soon as she had finished the task, Thornton immediately reclaimed her hand.

Thornton's touch quickly warmed her hand again. *They can stare all they want. My hand feels so warm and safe in Thornton's. I'm keeping it there, and my daughters can deal with it.*

CHAPTER FOURTEEN

December 14th

The sky was clear and bright with sunshine, which belied the mid-teen temperatures. The lake was frozen solid after weeks of nighttime temperatures in the single digits. The sun bounced off the ice, sending bright rays of light that outlined the tall evergreens.

Kate had risen early. She woke up, had a light breakfast in the dining room, and went back upstairs. She had a few phone calls to make before meeting with Karina Celeste.

Returning to the living room around eleven, Kate didn't see Karina downstairs. She checked the dining room but didn't find her, even though the previous day, during their conversation, they had agreed to meet at eleven in the living room.

The gorgeous sunshine reflected off the lake and caught Kate's attention. Moving over to the large picture window in the living room, she saw someone walking back from the lake. She quickly realized that it was the beautiful ballerina. Kate was always impressed with the way Karina seemed to glide along with every step. There was a subtle elegance to her.

Quickly putting on her coat, hat, and gloves, Kate stepped outside and met Karina before she returned inside the inn.

"Kate, it's gorgeous here. Being back, I now remember how lovely it is around the lake, and the town is charming. This would be a fantastic place to get away from the city. Maybe I'll buy a summer home here. I can get freezing weather in New York, but the summers are too hot. I recall that the summers are not as hot here in Maine."

Letting out a small laugh, Kate said, "Shush, or a realtor might overhear you, and they'd have several listings to show you this afternoon. But, if you are serious, I could ask Cassidy for someone she would recommend."

"I'm not ready to buy something just yet. I will be busy with the new dance studio, but when I'm ready, I'll ask for the referral."

"I know the car service to take you to the train in Portland doesn't leave Lakeview until late this afternoon. Do you still have time for a trip into town?"

Karina linked her arm through Kate's, and they headed to the parking lot where Cassidy's car was parked. Cassidy often lent her mother her car, so Kate felt like she had more freedom than always having to ask someone else for a ride. If she decided to move to Lakeview, she'd need to purchase a car. Maybe she'd ask Thornton to help her pick out a vehicle suitable for the winters in Maine.

Twenty minutes later, the two women were seated at The Perk with their coffees and salads topped with fresh grilled chicken and Green Goddess dressing.

Karina put down her fork and looked at Kate. "Thank you for the lunch invitation. I was so energized after last night's performance that I woke up early. I decided to pack most of my belongings so I'd have all day to enjoy my last few hours in Lakeview. Kate, what was on your mind?"

Kate hesitated for a moment. "I was glad to hear you say you might buy a summer place here in Lakeview. I'm considering selling my condo in the city and moving to the lake house Duncan and I built a few years ago. Currently, there are tenants in the house, but yesterday I informed the property management company that I won't be extending their lease. I haven't made my final decision yet, but I'm starting to line things up in that direction."

She decided now was the time to broach the subject she wanted to discuss. "I'll be more involved with the local theatre, and I was hoping to convince you to join us in organizing our summer program. If you stay here in the summers, you'll want to find a way to occupy your time. You can't just sit by the lake all summer. What do you think? Can I count on your participation if you're here this coming summer?"

"I haven't even decided to move here yet, and you're asking me to join your organization?" Karina tilted her head but smiled. "Of course, I'll help you. It's another reason to spend the entire summer here. That's a fantastic idea. Thank you for thinking of me."

The women talked for another hour and were ready to leave when Kate heard a familiar, yet unpleasant, voice. She turned toward the front of the café and saw the local gossip, Mrs. Lester, with a few women from the local knitting group.

Although several tables were available on the other side of the café, Mrs. Lester led her group to a table directly across from Kate's.

The group made so much noise that it was hard to ignore them. Kate was surprised to see Mrs. Lester wearing one of Trish's handmade Lakeview Christmas sweaters. Typically, Mrs. Lester dressed very plainly, with her hair pulled back in a tight bun. She reminded Kate of an old-fashioned librarian, but today she sported the sweater, little green tree earrings, and a skirt peeking out from under her coat, decorated with red and green ornaments along the scalloped hem. It was not how Kate remembered her.

Mrs. Lester sat down and pretended she had just noticed Kate. She jumped back up and walked over to their table. "Well, hello. I didn't expect to run into the two of you today. I thought you'd both be heading back to the Big Apple versus staying in our little town."

Kate spoke first. "Mrs. Lester, I'm not sure if you've met Karina Celeste, the prima ballerina. Did you attend one of her performances? They were beautiful, and I could go on, but I won't."

With a huff, Mrs. Lester responded. "I don't live under a rock, and everyone in town was at one of the two performances. Yes, it was wonderful. It's nice to meet you in person, Madam Karina Celeste. Your performance was flawless. We are fortunate to have you in our little town. Will you be staying long?"

Karina put on her best smile. "Thank you for the kind words. The local children made the performance truly special, and I thoroughly enjoyed every minute I spent working with them. Unfortunately, I have to leave Lakeview and return to the city. I'm leaving later this afternoon."

"Kate, I heard that the inn is closed to outside guests for two weeks. That's not normal for Cassidy to do. I also heard she was having renovations done. It seems like an odd time of year to do them. Over the holidays, she is typically fully booked. Why turn away the business? Is something wrong?"

Trying not to show her irritation, Kate decided to be socially polite. "Nothing's wrong. As a matter of fact, everything is perfect. The inn is fully booked," Kate quickly interjected to stop Mrs. Lester from gossiping.

To maintain her patience, Kate took a quick breath and continued. "As you're aware, my younger daughter, Jennifer, and her family recently returned from Europe, which inspired Cassidy to close the inn to outside guests and create a fantastic two-week event for our family and close friends. Holiday-themed events are planned for every day, and every inch of the inn is decorated to look like a winter wonderland. Cassidy has truly outdone herself. I feel fortunate to have this special season at the inn."

Mrs. Lester seemed to accept Kate's response, but she quickly resumed talking. Luckily, one of the women at her table called out, saying they were starving and wanted to order. Kate was grateful to the woman who interrupted Mrs. Lester. Somehow, that woman had a talent for getting under her skin.

To avoid another conversation with Mrs. Lester, Kate suggested to Karina they should leave. She had one more stop to make before heading back to the inn.

Walking across the street, Kate led the way into Crystal Lake Gifts.

"Oh, how lovely! I haven't had the chance to stop by here yet," Karina remarked as she looked around.

Trish saw the two women enter and immediately approached them. "Kate and Karina, how wonderful to see you. Can I help you with anything today?"

Speaking first, Kate said, "I have a special thank-you gift in mind for my friend Karina. One of your handmade Lakeview Christmas sweaters would be perfect. She's so petite that I'm not sure if she needs a small or extra small. Can you help us decide?"

"You don't need to buy me a gift. I've loved every minute of my stay in Lakeview." Karina smiled graciously.

Kate placed her hand lightly on Karina's arm. "I know I don't need to, but I would appreciate it if you'd allow me to buy you a gift. If not a sweater, then something else."

Trish led them to the display of Twelve Days of Christmas sweaters.

Karina gently ran her hand over several sweaters. "Oh, these are gorgeous and so soft! And look, each one is slightly different. Kate, if you insist on buying me something, I'd love to have one of these. It would be perfect with leggings for a casual night with my friends."

Karina found what she wanted, and the purchase was processed quickly and placed in a gift bag.

At the last minute, Karina asked Trish if she had any more of the lacy shawls, similar to the one she saw Kate wearing at last night's performance. Trish showed her what was available, and Karina decided on two gorgeous hand-knitted, off-white shawls.

"I'll get these into gift bags for you. Is there anything else I can help you with today?" Trish asked.

"I wish we had more time," Kate replied. "Karina needs to go back to the inn to finish packing, see if she can get these extra packages in her luggage, and I'm bringing her back into town. It was easier for the car service to pick her up in town. They're driving her to the train station in Portland, where she'll catch the train to Boston and finally, back to the city."

Goodbyes were exchanged as Kate and Karina walked to their car and drove back to the inn.

Two hours later, Kate waved farewell to her friend. "Safe travels. If everything goes according to plan, you should be home to sleep in your own bed tonight. Let's plan to catch up after the holidays." Kate blew a kiss into the air and watched as the car slowly drove down Main Street.

Kate drove back through Lakeview, and she was reminded of how charming the town looked, all decked out in its Christmas finery. As darkness set in, the Christmas lights glowed, the elaborate window displays shone brightly, the shops stayed open late, and people milled around, often stopping to chat with one another. Lakeview truly was at its finest during the holidays.

Feeling grateful to spend time with her family and friends, Kate returned to the inn. She wondered if Thornton was there. Perhaps she would invite him to share a cup of cocoa and sit by the fire.

When did the idea of spending time with Thornton become so important? she wondered.

CHAPTER FIFTEEN

December 15th

The renovations to Room #210 were complete, and the next morning, Kate decided to check it out. The last time she'd seen the room, it was a dusty jumble of boxes and discarded furniture.

When Kate opened the door, she paused. Although Cassidy had shared the plans for the room with her, Kate hadn't been prepared for the transformation. The walls were painted a soft yellow, and the large windows let sunlight fill the room. The hardwood floors had been refinished, and several rugs were placed in areas where toys were stored in large bins, just waiting for someone to sit down and play.

A cozy reading nook featured a cushioned window seat in an alcove beneath one of the larger windows. Bookshelves flanked the walls on either side of the seat. Kate reflected on how perfect it would be to sit and read with the children.

Stepping further into the room, Kate noticed three twin beds had been built into the wall, two portable cribs and a playpen were set up, and a wall of built-in cabinets filled with games, toys, and craft supplies.

An ensuite bathroom and a compact kitchenette were added to improve the room's functionality.

"What do you think, Mother?" Cassidy asked Kate when she entered the room.

"It's wonderful! You've thought of everything, and the timing is perfect. With all the children staying at the inn over the holidays and the weather dipping into the single digits, it's the ideal place for them to play. It feels like a wonderland for the children. Plus, I get to join them. It's the first time I'll have all my grandchildren under one roof, and they'll have other playmates to keep them company."

Cassidy smiled at her mother. "Thinking about it, five children will be here starting next week."

Kate turned around and looked at Cassidy. "Five children?"

Putting her hand in front of her, Cassidy raised a finger for each child as she listed their names. "My daughter, Katie. Amanda's daughter, Emma, Jennifer's daughter, Addie, and Dr. Foster's two children, Ellie, now eight, and their son, Elijah, who's three. That's enough children to start our own daycare."

"Yes, five is right," Kate responded. "It will be great to hear the sound of children here. It's been a long time since I've been around that many little ones at once, but I'm really looking forward to it. This room is perfect, and I can't wait."

Cassidy rearranged a few games and adjusted the pillows around the reading nook. "Let's go downstairs and have a mid-morning cup of coffee. I have a few minutes before I need to go to my office. Would you like to join me?"

"Of course," Kate said as she hugged her daughter.

"I love your hugs," Cassidy remarked, "but what was that about?"

Kate smiled and said, "You always think of everything to make people comfortable and love the inn. Now you've created the perfect place for children to play and be entertained, especially when the weather isn't suitable for going outside. You are the most thoughtful person I know, and I love you for it. Let's grab that coffee and enjoy a few minutes of mother-daughter time."

With that, the two women went downstairs, poured coffee from the carafe in the dining room, and moved to the living room, each choosing one of the high-backed chairs near the fireplace.

Amanda stopped by the living room. "Hello, you two."

She walked over to where Kate and Cassidy were seated. "Kate, how did you like the renovations to Room #210?"

"That's easy to answer," Kate replied. "It goes beyond my expectations, and I can't wait for the children to see it. It's like having their own playland right inside the inn."

Amanda linked her arm with Kate's and said, "If a Christmas snowstorm actually happens, the playroom might be helpful for more than one reason, especially since we don't have any available rooms for them to play in now that Thornton has extended his stay. Additionally, one of Jennifer's shipments arrived earlier than expected, and forty shipping boxes are now stored in the room Karina checked out of. It might feel a bit like Grand Central Station around here for a few days. Cassidy definitely made a smart choice to renovate the room when she did," Amanda said. "I watched the local news show earlier, and they mentioned that the storm would most likely blow out to the Atlantic after it hits Boston, but you never know."

Before Cassidy could answer, Amanda asked, "Cassidy, is there anything special you'd like me to do to prepare? Just in case?"

Cassidy's smile faded. "Peter and I went over our emergency plan spreadsheet yesterday, and he placed an additional order of food, wood, and goodies, just to be safe. The propane company topped off the generator last week. Can either of you think of anything else we need to consider that we haven't already discussed? There's still time to add items to my spreadsheet before it's too late. Anyone? Anything?"

Amanda smiled. "It's highly unlikely your spreadsheet is missing anything important, but I'll check with Peter before I go into town this afternoon. I need to mail a couple of packages. Can I bring either of you anything back from town?"

Both women said they were fine, but Cassidy was still clearly preoccupied with the potential weather forecast.

"I know what you're thinking, Cassidy," her mother said softly. "But the probability is low that the storm will continue to Lakeview. I've watched several weather reports over the past few days, and they all indicate that the storm will move out to the Atlantic before it ever reaches Maine. Besides, they don't call you the Queen of Preparedness for nothing. I feel confident you've covered everything, and we'll all be safe, well-fed, and enjoy our time together if we end up snowed in."

Placing her hand on her mother's arm, Cassidy said, "Thank you, Mother. I'm glad you'll be here with us instead of in the city if there's a blizzard. I feel safer with everyone under one roof. If we're together, what could possibly go wrong that we couldn't handle?"

Groaning aloud, Cassidy blurted out, "Did I just say that out loud? I don't want to jinx us, but I do feel well prepared should there be a storm. A normal snowstorm in Maine is something we're used to, but blizzards, high winds, and power outages are always concerning."

Cassidy got up from her chair, leaned over to her mother, and hugged her. "Another perk of having you here with us is enjoying quiet times like this together, but I need to get back to the office and return a few calls. Can I get you anything?"

Kate said she was fine. *I hope for Cassidy's sake the storm truly does blow out to sea,* she thought.

Kate sat by the fire, thinking about the past few weeks at the inn. During her brief time in Lakeview, she already felt more hopeful about her life. Although she still missed Duncan deeply, the pain had lessened slightly.

Kate was thrilled to have her daughter Jennifer, and her family back in the States, and she was delighted that they would stay at the inn until their new home was ready.

Getting to know her granddaughter, Addie, better had been a gift, and she planned to continue making up for the years when she had only seen her once or twice a year.

Coordinating the special performance of The Nutcracker and seeing how thrilled her family was with the backstage passes made Kate smile. She genuinely hoped Karina would consider moving to the lake and joining the theatre board. She would be a valuable asset in attracting other dance troupes to Lakeview.

She couldn't help but turn her thoughts next to Thornton. How had he become a focal point in such a short time? Although he'd always been a close friend, something had shifted recently. The incident when she almost fell off the ladder while decorating the tree, and again when he placed a light kiss on her lips at the bottom of the stairs, both had contributed to this change.

In addition, Thornton had comforted her in the living room when her emotions overwhelmed her. She had easily moved into his arms. And that kiss! They both thought they heard bells when, in reality, it was the front doorbell. Of course they were interrupted, and neither had the chance to discuss how they felt.

Being widowed once was more than most women could handle, yet she had been widowed twice. Although decades apart, the sum of the impact on how she felt about taking any romantic risk remained a heavy burden.

It took her years to fully recover from her first loss. But, over time, Duncan had entered her life and literally swept her off her feet. She thought back to the hospital's annual gala, where Duncan had asked her to dance with him. She'd never forget the Waltz and how he skillfully guided them around the dance floor. He was a fantastic dancer, and she felt several pairs of eyes watching them.

At the end of the dance, Duncan had dipped her backward, nearly causing her to lose her footing. He quickly caught her around the waist and pulled Kate close to his chest, lifting her slightly off the ground. Yes, he literally swept her off her feet.

Duncan told everyone that story and took credit for being the one who pulled down Kate's armor and helped her ride the amazing wave of love they shared.

But then, without warning, Duncan was gone, and the armor quickly grew back in place without Kate even noticing.

When Thornton had asked her what was holding her back from opening her heart, she knew it was the armor. She wasn't sure how to overcome its rigidity, and it was hard to explain to others. She knew Thornton wouldn't intentionally hurt her, but she was more worried about her ability to shed the amor and totally accept his love. Both of them could get hurt.

Kate sat for hours, reflecting on her life, her marriages, and her children. She was at a crossroads. Her life was in her hands, and she had to find her path forward. It was her choice—no one else's.

Rising to leave the cozy room and head upstairs, Thornton crossed her mind again. It was that kiss in the living room when they were interrupted by the doorbell. Kate suddenly realized that the bells, or sounds she heard, were from the armor falling, not the inn's front door. Once she let her guard down, the emotions came rushing in. Her feelings for Thornton were growing stronger.

Unconsciously, she placed her hands over her heart and whispered, "I might still be a bit confused, but there is also more clarity. Something sweet is starting between us. After all these years, it feels almost magical that my heart is opening up for Thornton and shifting from friendship to something more romantic… "Oh no! Did I say that out loud?" Kate whispered. "And I'm still talking out loud." She pressed her lips tightly and ran her finger across them as if to indicate they were now zipped shut.

She needed time to sort through her feelings. She and Thornton never had enough time to discuss their emotions fully. He briefly mentioned retiring in a few years. Did he have plans beyond retirement?

Kate still hadn't decided whether to sell her condo in the city. The realtor had returned her call, but Kate had yet to give her final approval to list it. There were still so many unanswered questions, yet no solid answers. Was she stalling?

The more she thought about it, the clearer her decision became. Kate now knew it was time to list her city condo. While she still had the courage, she pulled her phone from her pocket, found the realtor in her contacts, and placed the call. Listing the condo was the first step in deciding her future. She didn't have to create a spreadsheet like Cassidy did for major decisions, but checking things off her mental list was a good start.

When the realtor answered, Kate quickly said, "Hello, it's Kate Moore. We spoke last month about possibly listing my condo in the city. I'm ready to proceed with the sale if you want to represent me. Please email me the paperwork, and let's get started immediately."

After Kate hung up, she felt a little lighter, as if a weight had been lifted from her shoulders. It was time to call the local rental agent and confirm they had informed the tenants in her lake house that she would not be renewing their lease.

Kate checked off two things on her mental list and felt even better. However, the memory of Thornton kissing her in the living room resurfaced. While the kiss was delightful and made her feel young again, it also underscored her need to better navigate her complex emotions about Thornton and the prospect of a new romantic relationship.

CHAPTER SIXTEEN

December 16th

Christmas was now nine days away, yet the weather forecast remained uncertain about the path of the snowstorm approaching the Northeast. This kind of unpredictability in weather patterns during the winter months was not uncommon, but it was always somewhat unsettling.

Cassidy went to Room #210 to stock the book nook with a few new items. She had ordered several Christmas coloring books and large storybooks, which had arrived earlier this morning. Her goal was to unpack them and arrange them on the shelves. Then, she needed to gather those planning to head into town for The Santa Train, an annual event that usually sold out. Knowing this, Cassidy had bought tickets months in advance. Amanda, Jennifer, and she were taking the five children staying at the inn to the event.

It would be fun, but first, they had to gather the children and dress them warmly. Then they would pile into the van, safely in their various car seats, and try to contain their enthusiasm during the short ride into town. It would be much easier to manage once they got the children on the train and buckled into their seats.

Taking one last look around the beautiful room, Cassidy smiled and reminded herself of how it had looked just a few weeks ago. The transformation was incredible, and she couldn't have asked for anything more.

Cassidy hurried downstairs and heard the excited sounds of children. Amanda and Jennifer had already gathered the kids and buttoned the last coats as she walked into the living room.

In an effort to grab everyone's attention, Cassidy announced loudly, "Hello, everyone. Are we ready to go see Santa on the train?"

A loud response erupted from the children and their escorts.

"Okay. We have some rules, so pay attention. You are to stay with your buddy. Hold hands with your adult when walking and never leave your group. We have the inn's van out front waiting for us. Let's go!"

It still took nearly fifteen minutes to get everyone into the van, buckle them in their age-appropriate restraint seats, and get ready to leave.

At the last minute, Cassidy had to rush back inside the inn to retrieve a lost mitten. In her haste, she ran most of the way. She quickly entered the living room and scanned for the mitten, which was easy to spot since it was bright yellow.

As she picked it up and began to leave the room, something caught her attention. Pausing to look closer, Cassidy realized the Baby Jesus statuette was missing from the cradle. She examined the nativity set and the rest of the room, but it was nowhere to be found.

Realizing she didn't have time to search for the statuette, she made a mental note to look for it when she returned from the train ride.

On the way back to the van, she thought about how odd it was that the statuette was missing.

As Cassidy jumped back into the van, she exhaled loudly and glanced at Jack, who had kindly offered to drive and wait to take everyone back to the inn.

"You're a lifesaver, sweetheart. Driving for us and dropping us off right at the train platform saves us some confusion. We should be ready for you to pick us up in two hours, but I'll call when we're almost back to the station."

Jack smiled at his wife. "No problem. I can see the children's excitement, and I hope everyone has a great time."

As they pulled out of the inn's parking lot, Cassidy said, "Jack, the Baby Jesus is missing from the cradle in the nativity set. I didn't have time to do more than a quick look around, but it was nowhere to be seen. When we get back, maybe you can help me look for it."

Jack agreed, and they set off to visit Santa.

The local train station was decked out in colorful lights and festive displays, but nothing compared to the actual 1950s passenger train, which chugged into the station under steam power. Christmas music played through speakers, and of course, Santa Claus stood at the train's doorway, waving to everyone waiting to board.

For years, the town's mayor portrayed Santa, perfectly fitting the role. He never needed to stuff his costume with an extra pillow or wear a fake beard and consistently earned rave reviews.

The kids had all loved The Santa Train, but the afternoon trip had completely worn out the children. Peter had expected they would need to eat soon after their return and go to bed early, so he prepared a meal for them. Of course, he made their favorite dishes, mac and cheese and chicken fingers. The meal was sure to encourage them to eat without fussing.

That evening, only the adults were at dinner, and Peter had prepared a wonderful meal. Amanda set a beautiful table with Christmas-themed linens and dishes. The glow of candles created a cozy ambiance in the room.

The table was full of family and friends. It had been years since most of Kate's family was at the table together. She was happy they were joined by Sarah and Tom, Dr. Foster and Leah, and Thornton.

"What is that delicious aroma?" Sarah asked as soon as she walked into the dining room.

Sarah and Tom had joined them at dinner. Tom was getting around better with his crutches, and staying in the first-floor accessible suite made life so much easier for him.

Peter responded. "I thought we could all use a relaxing yet satisfying meal. I prepared lobster bisque, accompanied by a Caesar salad and my homemade dressing, and grilled lake trout with roasted vegetables. For dessert, there's a simple chocolate layer cake. I was fortunate to get fresh lake trout at the dock this morning. It's great that we have ice fishermen in the winter. I hope everyone enjoys their meal."

"Thank you, Peter," Tom said. "Your meals are fabulous. I'd also like to extend my thanks again to Cassidy and everyone who made our stay possible. Oh, and the bonus of Sarah being able to join in several of your CLC events also makes me feel better. I worried she'd be stuck inside throughout the holiday because of my limited mobility. This is turning out to be the best holiday ever. Who would have ever thought that breaking my leg would turn into an enjoyable holiday?"

Turning to give his wife a loving smile, Tom added, "Sarah, I know I gave you a hard time about staying here for two weeks until the contractors could finish our first-floor bathroom at home, but you were right. I have more flexibility and comfort here, and the food is the icing on the cake. And speaking of cake, Peter, chocolate layer cake is my favorite."

Peter raised his glass in a toast of thanks to those around the table. "I'm just lucky to be able to cook for all my friends and family. Cheers!"

After dinner, Peter and Amanda suggested that everyone head to the living room, where he already had a roaring fire going. Wine and after-dinner drinks were served, and the mood was relaxed.

Cassidy looked over at the nativity scene, which reminded her that one piece was missing. Addressing the group, she asked, "Has anyone noticed that the Baby Jesus is missing from the cradle?"

All eyes turned to the area where the antique nativity had been placed.

Amanda got up from her chair and approached the empty cradle. She bent down and looked around the area where the set was sitting. "You're right, Cassidy. Baby Jesus is missing. That's so odd. Where could the statuette have gone? Does anyone remember the last time they saw it?"

No one seemed to remember the last time they'd seen the baby in the cradle. After a quick search around the room, the missing baby still hadn't been found.

"Don't worry about it tonight," Cassidy said, forcing a smile. "Let's enjoy our drinks. I want to give everyone an update on the upcoming CLC events. I plan to search the inn in the morning for Baby Jesus. I'm sure the small statuette is around here somewhere. It's a mystery for now, but I think maybe one of the children thought it was a doll to play with, and it's in one of the bedrooms, so please take a look when you go to your rooms tonight, and I'll check the playroom in the morning."

The discussion shifted to the upcoming CLC events. As usual, Cassidy reviewed a detailed itinerary of the events. When she finished, the group was quiet, enjoying the fire and their drinks.

After the fun-filled day, everyone was tired, so most of the adults went to bed early. It was unusual for the inn to be so quiet so early in the evening. Cassidy and Jack took advantage of the peaceful time and snuggled together on the sofa as the embers in the fireplace died down.

Cassidy let out a sigh and snuggled closer to her husband. "So far, it's been worth all the planning and extra work. The CLC events have been a great deal of fun, and they've allowed us to spend quality time together as a family. This is what the holiday season was meant to be. I can't wait to see what the next week brings."

Turning her head to look at her husband, Cassidy noticed Jack was already asleep and snoring. *So much for our romantic evening.* Waking him up, they both stretched, yawned, and went upstairs.

The inn was now at rest for the night.

CHAPTER SEVENTEEN

December 17th

Thornton sat in his room, gazing out at the lake. He had been on video calls most of the morning and desperately needed a fresh cup of coffee and a snack. Although his room had a coffee maker and snacks, he also needed to stretch his legs, so he decided to go downstairs.

Before heading to the dining room, Thornton got lost in his thoughts. He felt uneasy about how he and Kate had left things the afternoon before the ballet performance. He wanted to—no, he needed to—talk to her.

It was clear to him that his feelings had shifted. After promising himself he would be a good friend to Kate, listen to her when she needed to talk, and be a shoulder to cry on, he now found himself stepping into the danger zone of romantic involvement.

The balance between being a good friend and something more was precarious. If he pushed too hard and she wasn't ready, he could alienate her, and that would break his heart.

Continuing to explore his emotions, Thornton quickly realized he was falling deeply in love with her. He envisioned

Kate as a life partner with whom he could share special moments, travel, family gatherings, and quiet evenings by the fireplace.

He needed to choose the right words to help her understand. He was a publisher, for goodness' sake. He should be able to find the right thing to say.

Realizing his thoughts were going in circles, he needed a distraction and headed downstairs. Maybe striking up a casual conversation with Peter, Cassidy, or Amanda would help him get out of his own mind. Unfortunately, he didn't see anyone around. He glanced at the schedule Cassidy had posted on the wall near the check-in desk. He noticed that another CLC event was happening in Lakeview, so most of the family would be in town. He wondered if Kate had joined them.

Thornton picked up the house phone and called Kate's room. He was surprised when she answered. A bit tentatively, he asked, "Kate, if you aren't busy, will you meet me in the living room? I'd like to talk, and maybe we can share a cup of coffee or cocoa."

There was a pause on the other end of the line before Kate responded. "Okay. I'll be right down."

Kate entered the living room but didn't sit down. Instead, she said she was making two cups of cocoa and would be right back.

She returned with two steaming cups of cocoa and sat across from Thornton. While she had been gone, he'd lit a fire in the fireplace, which already filled the room with warmth and coziness. The heat had already reached the chairs where they sat.

"Thank you for joining me," he said. "I've been on conference calls all morning, and I needed to stretch my legs and get something to re-energize me. This cocoa smells amazing."

Taking a sip, Thornton decided to extend the invitation while he had her undivided attention. "I have to go to New York City tomorrow. I'll only be there overnight. I need to check on the work at my condo. While I'm there, I want to pick up some more clothes now that I'm staying at the inn for another two weeks."

"Oh. I wasn't aware you'd be away," Kate responded. "Thanks for letting me know, and I hope you have a good trip." She briefly looked sad but quickly masked it with a smile. She sipped her drink and gazed at the brightly lit fire.

"Kate, I was wondering if you'd like to go with me? I've already checked with the hotel where I'm staying, and they have rooms available. I have two tickets to see the Rockettes, which my assistant gave me as a Christmas gift, and I'd feel bad if I didn't use them."

Picking up speed to ensure he didn't lose his nerve, Thornton continued. "I already have a driver scheduled to pick me up here and take me to the hotel in the city. The driver plans to be available for me as needed. We can visit the city, check into our hotel rooms, attend the show, have dinner, spend the night, and return the next day, or even extend our stay to shop or explore the sights. You know how amazing the city is when it's dressed in its holiday finery."

When Kate stayed silent, he asked, "What do you think?"

Before she could reply, her phone rang. It was Cassidy. Fearing something was wrong, she excused herself and left the room.

Thornton let out a long breath, one he hadn't realized he was holding. It had taken all his courage to ask Kate to join him in the city. She'd looked surprised, and a fleeting expression of doubt had crossed her face when he asked her, making him certain she would turn him down.

He could hear her on the phone but couldn't understand what she was saying. He hoped everything was okay with the CLC event. Meanwhile, waiting for Kate's response made him anxious—something he rarely felt. He wasn't sure how to handle it, and the high level of chocolate in the cocoa only added to his nervousness.

He took advantage of the time Kate was out of the room to consider what was causing his anxiety. He realized that her response carried considerable weight. If she rejected him, it would mean she was distancing herself from any further romantic involvement.

If Kate said yes, she would join him, he needed to be careful not to read too much into it. He desperately hoped she would say yes, not only to experiencing the sights of the Big Apple but also to deepening their relationship.

Thornton went to pick up his mug and realized his hands were sweating. He routinely made multi-million dollar deals and stayed calm, never recalling having sweaty hands. It was amazing what one woman could do to a man without even knowing it.

He hoped Kate would return to the room soon, or he'd have to take a walk outside in the freezing cold temperatures to cool off. He suddenly felt like a teenage boy waiting for his first date to open the front door, only to see the girl's father on the other side. Oh boy, did he ever have it bad!

Kate finished her call from Cassidy. Her daughter asked if she wanted to join the group for dinner in town, but she declined.

Taking her time to return to the living room, she replayed Thornton's invitation, which had been a surprise. Thoughts swirled in her mind. If she declined, this would be the first year she would miss the Rockettes' annual performance in decades. She loved the show, and it would be fantastic to see it again. But the invitation involved more than just the show, and that made her uneasy.

Kate decided to be honest with Thornton.

Sitting down in the chair across from him, she said, "Thornton, your invitation took me by surprise. I love the Rockettes and was disappointed to realize I would miss them this year. It's thoughtful of you to invite me, but I'm not sure it's a good idea."

By the creases on his face, it was clear to Kate that Thornton was trying to decide whether to accept her response or probe to find out why she wouldn't join him.

"Can I ask why you don't think it's a good idea?" Thornton asked, clearly opting for the latter.

Kate briefly paused and then responded. "I left the city to help deal with my memories and try to move on with my life. I'm concerned that I haven't yet been away long enough, and returning might impact my progress."

Thornton quickly interjected, "Or, on the other hand, it might help to go to the city for a short stay where you'll be busy every minute, have no time to dwell on the past, and return to Lakeview feeling refreshed. It might actually help."

Getting up from her chair, Kate walked to the picture window and looked out at the snow-covered lake. She weighed the pros and cons. Was she reading too much into the invitation? Was this a significant step forward in their relationship?

On the other hand, she realized the trip would give the two of them the time away from prying eyes at the inn, a chance to talk about their lives thoroughly, and maybe, just maybe, time to deepen what Kate was already feeling for Thornton.

"When is the performance?" Kate asked, hoping to buy time to further reflect on the situation.

"There is a time constraint. The tickets are for tomorrow evening's performance. We need to decide today. I'm sorry if that puts too much pressure on you." He continued, "I've already checked with my circle of friends to see if anyone could use the tickets, but on such short notice, no one was available, and I didn't want to waste the money my assistant paid for them. With the whole condo flooding situation, I need to return to the city anyway. I thought inviting you to the city with me was the perfect solution. We could put the tickets to good use and enjoy some time together in the Big Apple. Please say you'll join me."

Kate picked up her cell phone. "Cassidy called to let me know that the group had decided to stop in town to eat. Let me give her a quick call before they order their meal. She seems to have daily plans between now and Christmas, and I don't want to miss an event that she's counting on me to join."

Stepping out of the room to make the call, Kate explained the situation once Cassidy answered. She told her daughter she didn't want her trip to the city to interfere with any of the special CLC events Cassidy had planned.

Cassidy sounded surprised by Thornton's invitation and that her mother was seriously considering it. "Mother, I hope you don't mind if I ask, but does the invitation feel like more than just a casual request to you?"

"Yes, it does," Kate replied. "I weighed the pros and cons, and since Thornton and I rarely find time to be alone at the inn, I'm leaning toward going with him. I'd get to see one of my favorite performances, plus we'll see the Christmas Tree lighting, and maybe do a little shopping. And, of course, enjoy a fantastic meal somewhere. Thornton entertains clients and big-name authors frequently, so he knows the most fabulous places to dine and can usually secure a last-minute reservation. But I want your input. What do you think?"

"It sounds like you already made up your mind," Cassidy said. "But I appreciate you asking for my opinion. I agree with Thornton. It would be an excellent opportunity for the two of you to see a show, enjoy a wonderful dinner, do some sightseeing, and spend quality time discussing what seems like a potential shift in your friendship to something more romantic. And, you know how fond we are of Thornton, so there's no question about his integrity or how he's always been protective of you. Just in the past few weeks since you and he have been at the inn together, I've noticed a big difference in how often I hear you laugh, see you smile, and even, if I may say so, see a dreamy look in your eyes."

"I wasn't aware I had a dreamy look in my eyes. I'll have to do a better job of looking miserable," Kate joked.

"Mother, sometimes you're impossible. But if you want my approval, you have it." Then Cassidy quickly added, "I'm sorry to rush off, but I need to get back to the table. The waiter is taking our orders. I love you, and I think you know what the right thing to do is. Gotta run."

Before heading back to the living room, Kate took a moment to assess the situation and realized she was sure she wanted to accept the invitation. Some questions needed answers, emotions to explore, and, on the bright side, fun events to attend.

Kate sat back down on the sofa. "I've thought about your invitation. I think we both realize it's more than just going to a theater performance. It's a chance to spend quality time together and decide whether there's more to our friendship than what we've shared so far. While that worries me a little, I'm willing to try." She watched as the frown on Thornton's face vanished, replaced by his charming, broad grin. "Yes, Thornton, I'd love to accept your invitation to go back to the city, see the show, have dinner, do some shopping, and find time for the important conversation about how we both feel. Let's do this!"

"That's fantastic, Kate, and you're right. This trip is more than just sightseeing. It will give us the time we need alone to explore our feelings. I can't wait for tomorrow! I'll go upstairs to my room and make all the arrangements. I also have a conference call in an hour, so it might be a while before I get back to you with updates."

They stood up, agreeing to meet in the library as soon as Thornton had confirmed their plans. As he began to walk around Kate to leave the room, he paused, turned back, and kissed her. His lips lingered for a moment, then he pulled her closer and kissed her again, this time more passionately.

Kate looked up in surprise, her heart pounding. "What was that for?"

A big grin spread across Thornton's face again. "That's a placeholder for the beginning of what I plan to do later, if we get some privacy. I can't wait."

Standing alone in the room, Kate smiled. Her pulse was racing faster than usual, and she struggled to find the right word to describe how she felt. The first word that came to mind was 'giddy.' *Yes, that's it. I've entered my early sixties only to feel like a teenager again. I'm not sure if that's a good thing or a bad thing, but I'll enjoy it for now.*

Before leaving the room, Kate walked over to the large window again and gazed at the lake. Something about Crystal Lake Inn brought happiness and surprises to those who stayed there. Maybe she wouldn't want to move anywhere else. Perhaps she should consider staying here. It was worth thinking about. With those thoughts swirling in her mind, Kate went back upstairs to wait for Thornton to update her on their plans.

A little later, Thornton joined Kate in the library, where she had been sitting, finally able to enjoy the book she had first started on the train.

Looking up from her book, she asked, "Were you able to make the arrangements for our trip?"

With a huge smile on his face, Thornton approached Kate and sat next to her on the sofa. "Yes, all the arrangements are confirmed. The car service will pick us up at nine a.m. tomorrow, giving us enough time to have breakfast before we leave the inn. We'll arrive at our hotel in the afternoon, allowing us to check into our rooms and relax before meeting in the hotel lobby at five. Since it's rush hour, we need to account for additional travel time to get to the theater. Our tickets are for the evening performance at six o'clock."

Thornton stopped speaking. He didn't want to rush through the details like a nervous teenager, but couldn't help himself. "Dinner after the show will be at Lumani in the private dining room. I remember you enjoyed Mediterranean dishes, and Lumani offers the most delicious meal, Loup de Mer, which is sea bass served with rice and steamed broccoli. I called a friend earlier, and he knows the chef, so he was able to confirm our reservation and mentioned that the sea bass is fresh.”

Kate smiled. “It sounds perfect.”

“Also, we have the driver available for our entire trip, and he has our itinerary. If you want to go shopping, he’ll hold our bags until we return to the inn. What do you think?”

“You thought of everything,” Kate replied. “Now I need to go upstairs and pack. In the morning, I’ll be in the dining room by eight and ready to leave at nine. I don’t want to be late. I’ll say goodnight now.”

As Kate turned to leave the room, Thornton spoke up. “Kate, you didn’t think I’d let you go so easily. Did you notice that we’re alone? I can’t help but take advantage of the moment.”

Thornton opened his arms, inviting her in. “Kate, come here.” Once she stepped into his embrace, he wrapped his arms around her. Their faces were only inches apart. Thornton could feel her breath on his face and noticed a light blush on her cheeks.

“I’ve been waiting all day to get you alone so I could do this.” With that, he pulled Kate even closer and captured her lips. They kissed several times—first a gentle exploration, then teasing. As his passion grew and he kissed her deeper, Kate responded. He knew it was time to regain his senses when he felt his heart racing and Kate’s quick heartbeat against his chest.

When the kiss ended, Thornton pulled back slightly to get a better look at Kate’s face. He noticed she was smiling. “Why the smile? I was hoping for something a little dreamier.”

"It's just like a man to expect his kisses to bring on a dreamy look," she teased. "Actually, my smile means I was thoroughly satisfied. It's been a while since I've experienced these emotions."

Kate stayed in his embrace. "Do I feel dreamy? Yes. But I'm also ready to feel a deeper emotion. That realization is what made me smile. You know, you are an excellent kisser."

Now it was Thornton's turn to smile. "I've had years of practice. I'm glad you approved. You are very kissable."

Kate asked, "Is kissable even a word?"

"Of course it is. Many of our romance authors use it. You see, I have the advantage of reading twenty or thirty romance novels every year. I've learned a lot from them. Just wait to see what other tricks I have up my sleeve."

While they remained in each other's arms, Thornton leaned into Kate and planted a tender kiss on her cheek. "I'd better say goodnight before I get carried away."

Kate replied, "Yes, we'd better end our make-out session. By the way, do adults our age still call it making out? I'm out of touch with slang, but I still love using it sometimes."

Thornton shook his head, smiling, dropped his arms, and walked across the room to the door. He turned around, gallantly bowed, and said goodnight one more time before leaving the room.

Kate felt the need to sit down quickly to assess her feelings better. She wanted to savor the dreamy sensation, as Thornton had described it. Didn't Cassidy mention she saw a dreamy look, also? *I'm not sure about dreamy, but I know that I'm tingling all over.*

Thornton had awakened feelings and emotions she had buried years ago when Duncan died. As wonderful as uncovering her emotions was, she still had some reservations about where she and Thornton were headed.

She turned around when she heard someone enter the room. She had briefly hoped it was Thornton, but she quickly realized it was Cassidy. The group had returned from their long day in town, put the children to bed, and was winding down for the night.

"Mother, I saw Thornton going upstairs to his room. I wanted to check if you're ready for the trip. Is there anything I can do to help?"

When Kate turned to face Cassidy, her daughter immediately sat beside her and took her hand. "Mother, your cheeks are flushed, and I can feel your pulse racing. Are you okay?"

Now, Kate felt embarrassed. "Of course I'm fine, but I feel a little like a teenager after her first make-out session. Oh, is that too much information to share with my daughter?"

Cassidy reflected on this new information. Clearly, this relationship was going faster than she expected. She was protective of her mother, probably too much so at times. *But then again, so is Thornton,* she mused. Was her mother moving too fast? *Well, she is in her sixties,* Cassidy reminded herself. And a light bulb went off. *Mother is a big girl, and if Thornton makes her happy, who am I to stand in the way?* Cassidy decided she wouldn't share this latest juicy tidbit with her sister Jennifer. *She'll find out eventually.* Cassidy smiled.

"No, it's not TMI, Mother," she replied. "I'm so happy you're waking up to a new relationship and experiencing those first moments of joy and intimacy again. I would usually worry about any new relationship you started, but not with Thornton. I know he respects you, and I can see in his eyes that he's getting serious when he looks at you. Your trip to the city is the perfect opportunity for you two to be alone, discuss your futures, ensure your plans align, and see where this relationship is headed."

"Thank you, dear," Kate said quietly. "I'm so fortunate to have a daughter I can talk to about anything."

Trying to stifle a yawn, Cassidy added, "I'm exhausted after our outing today. I'm heading to bed now since it's getting late, and you should go to bed too. You have a busy day tomorrow."

Kate stood up, and when Cassidy also rose, Kate reached over and embraced her daughter. "You are the best daughter any mother could ask for. You've made it so easy to openly discuss my potential feelings with you. Along with your support and Jennifer's, it means the world to me."

"I'm certain Jennifer will come around like I did, but it might take her a little longer since she doesn't know Thornton as well as I do, and she's even more pragmatic than me.

Kate raised an eyebrow at that comment, and the two laughed. Then they quietly headed up the stairs so they wouldn't disturb anyone who was asleep. They paused at the door to Kate's room and shared another hug. Cassidy then continued to her room.

Once Kate slipped into her room, she headed straight for the window. It was too dark to see the lake, but she looked up and saw a stunning display of stars and a bright moon. She quietly prayed to heaven, asking if she was making the right choice. Though she didn't expect a direct answer, she suddenly felt a warm sensation on her arms. She was sure it was Duncan encouraging her to move forward with her life.

Quickly getting ready for bed, Kate set her phone alarm for an early start so she could finish packing and have time for breakfast. Now, she needed to fall asleep.

Finally, thirty minutes later, after tossing and turning, she realized what had been troubling her and causing her so many mixed emotions. She sat up in bed and looked down at the ring finger on her left hand and the stunning diamond wedding set Duncan had given her.

Unsure why it suddenly occurred to her that it might be time to remove them, Kate got out of bed and walked over to the dressing table. She hesitated before taking off the rings. Eventually, she pulled them off, kissed them, and placed them in her jewelry box.

It felt right. She returned to bed and quickly fell into a peaceful sleep.

CHAPTER EIGHTEEN

December 18th

Kate and Thornton discussed the show as they walked the two blocks from the Rockettes' performance to their restaurant. They both enjoyed it, and even though it was similar every year, subtle changes always kept it fresh and engaging. The dancers were talented, and the audience was always enthusiastic in their applause.

Having never visited Lumani before, after Thornton mentioned it was where they would have dinner, Kate did some online research on the restaurant. It received high ratings. She felt relieved he didn't take them to one of her favorite restaurants in the city, as that would bring back too many painful memories with Duncan.

They had time before their dinner reservation to walk the short distance to Rockefeller Center and see the magnificent Christmas tree, which was a spectacular sight this year.

Thornton enjoyed learning the story behind the donated tree each year and shared it with Kate. "It's a seventy-four-foot-tall Norway Spruce. It isn't the tallest tree to earn the honor of being the annual New York City Christmas Tree.

The tallest has been one hundred feet tall. However, this year's tree, with an impressive width of forty-three feet, looks enormous. The tree is seventy-five years old. It's wrapped in over fifty thousand multi-colored LED lights. If that's not enough, the star on top is three-dimensional, with seventy spikes covered in Swarovski Crystals."

Pausing to let the information sink in, he continued. "Do you know what happens to the tree once it's taken down?"

Kate shook her head to indicate no.

"The tree is donated to the city, and the lumber is donated to Habitat for Humanity. It's a win/win. Visitors get to enjoy it, and then the proceeds go toward building a home for a deserving family. Patterson Publishing is also proud to support Habitat for Humanity."

"Thank you for sharing that information with me. All the years I lived in the city and visited the tree lighting, I didn't know those details. You'd make a fantastic tour guide."

Thornton gave Kate a big smile. "I think I'll stick with publishing. It can be frustrating, but I love working with authors, especially new writers who have enough talent to surprise us all and instantly make the bestseller list with their first book."

The evening was chilly, but they were dressed for the cold. Thornton asked Kate if she wanted the driver to pick them up and take them to the restaurant, but she preferred to walk. She had worn sensible shoes and dressed warmly, wanting to enjoy the holiday decorations on their way to the restaurant.

It was almost nine o'clock, yet the restaurant was still crowded, and the line for walk-ins was long. When Thornton checked in with the hostess, they were promptly taken to their seats in the private dining room. This room was smaller, with about a dozen tables, dim lighting, candles, and soft music playing from overhead speakers.

"The room is lovely," Kate said.

Thornton responded, "I've been to the restaurant once before, but it was in one of the large dining rooms. It was nice, but not as comfortable as this more intimate setting. I'm glad you like it."

The meal lived up to everything Thornton and the reviews promised. The food was delicious, the service impeccable, and the company delightful. Thornton had plenty of interesting stories to share, many of which were humorous.

As Thornton had instructed, the driver picked them up two hours later to take them to the hotel. Kate offered to walk, but Thornton insisted the driver pick them up. He said the wind had picked up, and given the late hour, he would feel better returning to the hotel in the car.

As Kate entered the hotel lobby, she felt uncertain about what to say. However, Thornton quickly asked if she would like a nightcap, and she agreed.

The server at the hotel bar presented the options available. Kate ordered decaf chamomile tea, while Thornton chose a snifter of top-shelf Cognac. It was clear to Kate that Thornton knew his brandy well. She decided to remember which brand he had selected so she could ask Peter to stock it for special occasions.

The server promptly returned with their drinks and left them to chat.

Kate was still on cloud nine from the Rockettes' amazing performance, the delicious dinner, and the city's sights. However, it was apparently all starting to catch up with her. She fought hard to hide a yawn, but Thornton noticed it.

"I saw that yawn," Thornton softly said. "I guess it's not a good time to discuss our situation. I want you wide awake and coherent. Let's shelve the discussion until morning."

Kate smiled, "Thank you for understanding. I'm not used to these late nights anymore, even though it's only midnight. I promise I'll be ready for our talk in the morning. Let's meet for breakfast. I noticed a lovely window table in the dining room earlier when we passed by. I'll plan to come downstairs early to see if we can sit there. It's set apart from the other tables so we can talk freely."

"That would be great." Thornton reached for Kate's coat and headed to the elevators.

They were on the same floor but at opposite ends of the hallway. Thornton's room was closer to the elevators, yet he still insisted on walking Kate to her door.

Standing in the ornate, dimly lit hallway of the historic hotel, Kate rummaged through her bag to find her room key. "Thornton, you didn't have to walk me to my room, but it was very gentlemanly of you." She paused, unsure of what to say next.

Kate waved her room key over the door sensor and heard it click. She gently pushed the door open so it wouldn't automatically relock. Turning toward Thornton to say a final goodnight, she paused. She felt drawn to him. She reached out, hugged Thornton, then pulled back slightly and kissed him on the cheek.

Thornton stopped her from entering her room by pulling her back into an embrace. Kate felt safe, yet slightly vulnerable in his arms, but the longing was there for something more. She wondered if she'd lost all her senses, including her sense of what was proper. Did she even know what she should do? She thought to herself, *Am I crazy? Am I ready for something more serious?*

Kate noticed Thornton's questioning look. She had to decide quickly. Should she invite him into her room, or would things go further than she was prepared for? *This was the moment of truth.*

"I'm sorry, Thornton. I'm exhausted, and I fear I'm caught up in the excitement of the evening, which was extraordinary. Let's call it a night. I'll see you for breakfast in the morning."

Kate turned and stepped into her room, smiling one last time at Thornton. She blew him a quick air kiss and shut the door behind her. The last thing she saw as the door closed was Thornton still standing there. Though he didn't look upset, he did seem a little sad.

Once Kate closed the door, she leaned against it. She kicked off her shoes and stood there, feeling like she might crumble into a ball on the floor if she let her emotions take over. What was she thinking? She knew—she was thinking about how good it would feel to be in Thornton's arms, to have him hold her tightly against his chest, and… to kiss her.

Yes, she remembered their few brief kisses back at the inn, but she would only be fooling herself if she denied that she wanted more. And she knew he did.

Oh no—she was definitely in trouble. Now what?

As luck would have it, Thornton called Kate at seven o'clock the next morning to inform her of another issue at his condo, as well as a matter that required immediate attention at the office. He told her he couldn't join her for breakfast, but he would meet her in the hotel lobby at ten o'clock. That would still give them time to return to Lakeview and join the others for that day's CLC event.

After Kate hung up from her call with Thornton, she felt relieved that they wouldn't be discussing their relationship this morning. However, she still felt torn. She knew Thornton's other issues gave her three extra hours to figure out what she wanted to say to him. That should be enough time to think things through and prepare for their ride back to Lakeview.

Thinking more about it, Kate realized she wasn't sure whether three hours or even three days would suffice to fix the many issues swirling in her mind. After last night, she knew she wanted more from their relationship. The armor was falling away, and quickly. Still, something was holding her back, and her doubts kept lurking. What could it be?

CHAPTER NINETEEN

December 19th

Cassidy was excited about today's CLC event, an afternoon of ice skating at the Lakeview Ice Rink, where she had become good friends with the owner, Abby Roark.

Abby was an Olympic gold medal ice skater who retired from professional skating a few years ago due to an injury. When the rink's former owners decided to retire, the community feared it would be shut down. However, Abby stepped up to save the rink, which she had visited many times while spending holidays with her grandparents.

Being known as the first female to complete a Quad Axel with four-and-a-half rotations, Abby's fame quickly grew, along with the demands on her time. This included her professional competitions and performances with international touring groups. Fatigue and an unfortunate fall ended her competitive career, but after a few months of rehabilitation, she was back on the ice, had purchased the rink, and moved to Lakeview.

Cassidy recalled the moment she first met Abby at a meeting of the Lakeview Merchants' Association. She remembered watching the attractive woman walk into the room, appearing uneasy. She opted to take a seat in the back. Strikingly beautiful, Abby had long blonde hair and large hazel eyes. Tall with long legs, she seemed familiar, but Cassidy couldn't immediately place this new face. Once Cassidy noticed how gracefully the woman walked and sat down, she wondered if this was Abby Roark, the former Olympic skater and new owner of the rink. A quick Google search confirmed it.

After the meeting, Cassidy had invited Abby for coffee at The Perk, and the rest was history. Abby frequently met with Cassidy and her friends for coffee or Sunday brunch at the inn.

Since establishing herself in the community by offering skating lessons during the winter and participating in special holiday events, Abby purchased a house near the lake, indicating she was here to stay.

Over the past two years, the Lakeview Christmas calendar had added special holiday events at the rink. This year, Cassidy worked with Abby to find an afternoon when she could rent the rink for one of her CLC events. While there would still be others at the rink, overall attendance would be lower, making it a safer time for even the younger children to skate.

Cassidy was amazed by the walker-like devices they now had for children to skate safely. She wished they had been available when she was younger. She learned to skate by falling a lot and getting back up, only to fall again.

An article in the *Lakeview Gazette* about Abby's career provided insight into what drew her to the sport. Besides growing up in Maine and Wisconsin, where the winters were long and the lakes frozen, allowing for safe skating for several months each year, she fell deeper in love with the sport as she became more accomplished.

The article quoted Abby as saying, "Skating professionally is much more work than most people realize. The daily practice, working with nutritionists to maximize energy, costume fittings, hair and makeup techniques, taking care of skates, and traveling, all take a toll on skaters. But, on the other hand, there's nothing like gliding across the ice. It's almost magical, and everything else around you disappears."

The article continued, "When I added more complex jumps to my waltz routines, it was exhilarating when I nailed one. The first time I tried the four-and-a-half Quad Axle, I failed so badly that I twisted my ankle and had to stay off the ice for two weeks. But I was determined to nail it. I felt it was within my reach if I trained hard enough. After failing at it hundreds of times, the first time I succeeded, I sat down on the ice and cried."

Cassidy could relate to the feeling that you could do anything if you tried hard enough. When she first bought the crumbling inn, she knew she could make it successful, but the first couple of winters when she'd booked only a few reservations had her second-guessing her ability to run a business.

Once she put on her marketing hat and offered special winter and holiday packages, her business became sustainable year-round. Now, she was routinely booked solid. Recently, she had been considering the potential of expanding the inn. She owned several acres of land adjacent to the current structure and had the space to add more rooms.

She ruminated as she skated to the music around the rink. Was she ready to take a whole new expansion on? Life was finally settling down to a nice pace. Was she prepared to upset things?

Her thoughts were interrupted as her mother glided past her on the ice. Growing up in Maine, Kate, Cassidy, and Jennifer were excellent skaters. Since Abby was busy working with the children, Cassidy had a few minutes of free time to demonstrate her skating skills.

She sped up, passed her mother, and turned around to tease her. "See, I can still outskate you, Mother," Cassidy said. Kate laughed and linked arms with Jennifer, who hadn't skated in several years and needed a refresher before tackling anything more complicated.

Cassidy turned back around and picked up speed. Once clear of the other skaters, she jumped into the air, performed a split, and then returned to the ice to execute a quick spin. When she finished, she heard applause from the sidelines.

The applause came from Thornton and Jack, who finally arrived at the rink. They'd been delayed because Thornton had to finish an important video call with the Board of Patterson Publishing, which was shutting down for the holidays. Jack hurried to put on his skates so he could join Cassidy on the ice.

Thornton wasn't an experienced skater. He had hesitated to come to the rink, but Jack insisted he could sit on the sidelines and cheer for the others.

Once Kate saw Thornton, she approached the rail that separated the ice from the seating area. "We put a pair of skates in your size under the bench. I was hoping you would join us on the ice."

"Kate, I'm a city boy and didn't have the chance to glide across the ice frequently like you did. I'd make a fool of myself if I went out there."

Around that time, Abby returned the children to their parents. She overheard the conversation and skated over to Thornton. "I'd be happy to give you a few pointers. Put on your skates and come join us."

Thornton wasn't entirely convinced, but he decided to put on the skates and see if, with Abby's help, he could at least stay upright on the ice.

Abby took his hand and helped him onto the ice. Kate skated away, leaving Thornton to his private lesson.

Ten minutes later, Abby had Thornton moving along the rail, steadier but still at a slow pace.

Kate skated up next to Thornton and grabbed his hand, telling Abby she was free to help other skaters who stood on the sidelines with looks of anticipation.

"I'll take it from here. Come on, Thornton, let me guide you around the outer edges of the rink. That way we'll stay out of the traffic."

The two skated for several minutes. Still wobbly but gaining confidence, Thornton could now talk to Kate while skating. "This isn't so bad. I'm starting to enjoy the feeling of gliding along. Thanks for having patience with me."

As soon as he said those words, he lost his balance and fell onto the ice, taking Kate down with him. Of course, they ended up lying on the ice in each other's arms. Cassidy and Abby saw them fall and rushed over to help, making sure they weren't hurt.

Once they caught their breath, Thornton and Kate began to laugh. They laughed so hard that Cassidy and Abby struggled to get them back on their feet.

Cassidy asked, "Is everyone okay? Can you skate off the ice so we can have a good look at you?"

Standing fully upright, both Kate and Thornton said they were fine, but they chose to move off the ice and sit on the benches along the outer edge of the rink's railing.

Cassidy asked Jennier and Abby to watch the children, and she got hot cocoa for her mother and Thornton. She sat with them for a few minutes. Soon, her mother and Thornton were laughing about past mishaps, especially from their college days.

Realizing she wasn't needed, Cassidy went back to skating and enjoyed her time with the children. Everyone was having a fun afternoon.

Jennifer skated over to Cassidy. "Hey, sis, look at those two over there. They seem to be having a great time, even after that hard fall. I'm glad to see Mother so happy. Coming home to Lakeview was definitely the right choice for her. I'm glad you encouraged her to spend the holidays with the family. Even if Mother denies it, something is going on between her and Thornton, I just know it."

Seeing the concern on her sister's face, Cassidy asked, "Jennifer, would you mind if something deeper was going on between those two? You don't know Thornton as well as Jack and I do, so I could understand if you had some reservations."

"At first, I didn't think Mother was ready for another romantic relationship, but the more I see her and Thornton together, and the more time he spends with us, the more I become comfortable with the idea that something more is developing." Jennifer put a gloved hand to her chin in thought. "I think the only barrier is Mother herself. While she's displaying all the signs of wanting something more, I don't think she's quite ready to admit it yet. Something is holding her back."

The two women stopped talking when they heard their mother giggling. Looking at each other, Cassidy and Jennifer started to laugh. "Listen to our Mother. She's giggling like a teenager," Jennier said. Looking around at the others from their party, several other pairs of eyes glanced toward Kate and Thornton.

Cassidy whispered to her sister, "I think you're right, and the only person here today who isn't aware that something is brewing between those two is our mother. Let's hope she finally lets her guard down and gives Thornton the chance he deserves and the relationship she needs to move forward with her life."

Before Cassidy could say more, they heard the music change, and the staff asked everyone to step behind the rail. Abby had agreed to a short performance for the group.

Standing in the center of the rink, Abby struck a pose with both arms raised toward the sky. As the music shifted to a waltz, she pushed off with her left skate and quickly followed with her right. It only took a few steps before she sped around the ice, twirling and forming large interconnected circles. After gaining speed, Abby rushed halfway down the rink, pushed herself into the air, and completed three spins before gracefully landing back on the ice. Before the song ended, she made several more passes around the rink, finally returning to the center, twirling so fast that it was hard to keep track of her revolutions. Her arms gradually rose above her head before stopping abruptly at the exact moment the music ended.

Those gathered were in awe of Abby's performance. It was graceful, executed perfectly, and reminded them that a Gold Medalist had just given them a private peek into her capabilities without even breaking a sweat.

Cheers and applause erupted as Abby displayed several curtsies for the audience. Finally, she took the time to take selfies with the children. Cassidy hadn't anticipated the special performance or the selfies, but she was grateful for both.

Abby was a true professional, yet she remained down-to-earth and approachable, winning the hearts of the entire community. They were lucky she chose Lakeview as her home.

Cassidy realized that not everyone had the opportunity to join in these types of experiences. It reminded her once again why Lakeview was the best place to live, and she couldn't imagine living anywhere else.

She glanced across the ice to see Thornton put his arm around her mother. Yes, something was brewing between those two, and she couldn't wait to see where it went. If it meant she'd see more smiles from her mother and less indecision, she was all for it.

CHAPTER TWENTY

December 20th

Christmas was only five days away. The local shops in Lakeview were crowded and were about to get even more so as schools were starting their holiday break the next day. Church choirs were practicing for holiday concerts. Overnight, weather forecasters mentioned the possibility of a storm moving into the southern tip of Maine before heading out to the Atlantic Ocean.

During breakfast at the inn, everyone buzzed about the updated weather forecast. Although no significant snowfall was predicted for Lakeview, most longtime Mainers had seen this type of Nor'easter before. They knew to stay prepared for a last-minute shift in the storm's path. The storm could blow out to sea earlier than expected or head straight up the coast toward Lakeview.

Trish had left the inn well before seven that morning. To better accommodate the large crowds, the gift shop had extended its hours. Her husband, Derrick, had a rare chance to have breakfast with the others, which didn't happen often, and he was taking full advantage of the buffet Peter arranged for the extra guests.

Derrick was the last to fill his plate. Once he sat down, Peter spoke up. "Derrick, what do you think about the updated forecast? Should we prepare for heavy snow on Christmas?"

"You never know with these Nor'easters, but I have to take the potential seriously. I've scheduled a meeting with my staff for later this morning. We need to be prepared just in case. Regrettably, this could mean longer shift hours than usual for our team, which would negatively affect their celebration plans. I feel bad about that, but it can't be helped."

Derrick continued, "The mayor also asked for a special meeting of the Lakeview Town Council later today. He wants everyone to be ready in case he calls for a Weather Emergency. I hope it doesn't come to that. I was looking forward to a relaxing twenty-four hours between Christmas Eve and Christmas Day evening. I'm scheduled to be off, but if the weather changes, I'll be on duty and in town."

Peter looked around the table at the others who could be negatively impacted if the storm forecast for their area changed.

He looked further down the table and saw that Dr. Foster was staring intently at his phone screen. "Dr. Foster, is the hospital gearing up for a potential storm?"

Looking up from his phone when he heard his name called, Dr. Foster responded. "Yes. We had a meeting about it yesterday. The hospital has a certain number of staff we need to operate safely, and with the large number of vacation days already scheduled, it could be difficult if we get hit hard."

He took a sip of his coffee. "Like Derrick, I was hoping to have extra time off over the holidays, but babies don't seem to care about snowstorms when they decide to enter this world. I'm very thankful that Cassidy invited us to join the fun at the inn. I won't worry as much since Leah and the children are here with all of you. I know they'll be in good hands."

Cassidy finally spoke up, "I'm also hoping the storm blows out to sea before it reaches us, but in case we get hit, I'm glad we're all under one roof. But, I'm also responsible for the fact that we are all here together, which means I plan to be as prepared as possible, just in case."

Peter took note of the comments about being prepared. "In case some of you aren't aware, Cassidy is known as the Queen of Preparedness. We already had a detailed spreadsheet of additional items we ordered for the CLC events and to handle a full house. When the first mention of a possible Nor'easter came up, Cassidy pulled me and Amanda into a meeting to add more wood, extra fuel for the generators, and enough food to feed most of Lakeview. I estimate that we can run on generator power for nearly two weeks. We've never been without electricity for longer than a few days, so I believe we truly are prepared."

Cassidy replied, "Okay, you can make fun of me now, but when you stay warm and well-fed if the power goes out, you'll know who to thank."

Peter started clapping, and the room burst into applause. "Here, here, to our Queen. All kidding aside,

Cassidy. We truly appreciate all your efforts to keep us safe, warm, and fed."

Kate walked into the room and asked what the applause was for. She had been upstairs in Room #210, reading a Christmas story to the children who had eaten earlier. "I only heard the last part of Cassidy's statement, but I feel safe because of all her planning. Besides, I think everyone is overreacting to the potential storm. It snows all the time in this part of Maine. So far, I've only heard about a couple of inches of snow, and Mainers are tougher than that. No one has said the word 'blizzard' yet."

There was a gasp across the room. Cassidy spoke up first, "Mother, we don't typically use the word blizzard unless the weather people use it first. You know how superstitious Mainers can be. Let's stick with snowstorm for now."

Kate said, "Much to do about nothing if you ask me."

Wanting to lighten the mood, Peter grabbed the coffee carafe from the side table and started refilling cups while sharing a funny story about a fifty-pound bag of flour exploding in the kitchen just minutes before the health inspector arrived a few years earlier. However, he could tell that some people around the table were secretly worried about the coming storm.

Right after breakfast, Jack and Thornton met in the library to talk about Jack's current manuscript.

Jack provided an update. "I've hit all the target dates from your team. Staying on track is much easier thanks to the detailed outline and the timeline they provided. This book is flowing more easily than my last one. I don't know if it's because I'm more experienced, or your team's involvement is clearing out obstacles. Either way, I appreciate the help."

Thornton smiled. "Let's say it's because you're a great writer and leave it at that. As long as you stay on track, we can both enjoy some downtime over the Christmas holiday. I'm looking forward to being part of a traditional celebration this year."

Jack quickly cut in. "There's nothing traditional about what Cassidy's created here at the inn this year. This more closely resembles a Hallmark Christmas movie on steroids, but I'm also enjoying it, so that's not a complaint."

Opening his briefcase, Thornton pulled out some folders and placed them on the table.

Jack had been wanting to discuss a subject with Thornton for a few days, but so far, he had hesitated to do so, and now seemed like a good time to bring it up. The topic was Kate.

"Thornton, if you have a few more minutes, I'd like to speak with you about something."

Thornton continued looking through the report in front of him without glancing up at Jack. "Okay, what's on your mind?"

Jack needed Thornton's full attention, so he blurted out the topic. "I'd like to talk about your relationship with Kate."

Thornton slowly placed the report on the table and frowned. "Okay. What's on your mind?"

Jack chose his words carefully. "I don't mean to overstep, but we're all connected because you represent my books, and

Kate is my mother-in-law. Cassidy and I have noticed that you and Kate seem closer than before. While you've always been good friends, something has changed. If you two were to move into a serious relationship and things went badly, it would be an uncomfortable situation for all of us. And Kate is just now starting to recover from losing Duncan. I don't want to think about losing you as a publisher or a friend, but I also don't want to see Kate get hurt. She's a very special person, and I care about her deeply. She's been like my second mother these past few years."

"Jack, I appreciate that you felt comfortable bringing up the topic. I've also wanted to talk to you about it, but it never felt like the right time."

Jack quickly said, "Well, now that I've opened the door, let's discuss it."

"Yes, I do have feelings for Kate," Thornton said, a smile lighting up his face. "I've always had some level of feelings for her going back decades, but I never acted on them, and I lost my chance with her two different times. When we found ourselves together on the train, something in my heart opened up, and I knew I couldn't let her walk out of my life again."

"So, what's holding you back now?" Jack asked.

"I think Kate feels the same way about me and about not missing our current chance, but…well, it's not me holding us back. I can tell something is holding her back. I plan to spend the rest of my time here convincing her that we could have a wonderful next chapter. I'd appreciate it if you'd keep this to yourself for now. I don't want to push her, but I think she needs a little more time to realize how deeply she feels for me."

Jack agreed to keep Thornton's feelings for Kate to himself a little longer. He hoped Cassidy didn't flat-out ask him if he had talked to Thornton about it. He never lied to his wife, yet he never lied to Thornton either. It was going to be an interesting Christmas.

Cassidy sat in her office while the inn stayed quiet, working on invoices and payroll. These tasks weren't her favorites, but they were necessary to keep the inn running smoothly. She was finishing up her work when someone knocked.

Sarah opened the door. "Do you have a few minutes for an update on the quilt?"

Cassidy quickly closed her laptop. "Come on in and have a seat. Of course, I want to hear what you've found out."

For the next few minutes, Sarah shared the news. "The article in *Quilters' Quarterly Magazine* turned out to be helpful. A woman named Marie Boothby responded, saying she believed the quilt might be a long-lost treasure of her great-grandmother."

"Sarah, did you speak to this person? Did she have the details about the quilt we didn't include in the magazine article?"

"Yes. She knew the quilt had a scalloped edge made of red and green fabric. Better yet, she has an old deed showing that her great-grandparents were the original owners of this inn. While she couldn't confirm how the quilt ended up behind a wall, as a child, she had heard stories of secret doors and hidden compartments. Unfortunately, because of the Great Depression, the family was forced to sell the inn, which they had previously used as a summer and holiday retreat. They moved all their belongings to their primary residence in Boston and had always hoped to repurchase it, but her great-grandfather died of a massive heart attack soon after they returned to Boston."

Cassidy asked, "Did she tell you anything else?"

"Ms. Boothby went on to say that period had been painful for the family, so they rarely talked about it, except to say the Boothby family was one of the original settlers in Lakeview. She has never been to Lakeview, but she'd love to see the home her great-grandfather built."

Pulling up a picture on her phone, Sarah forwarded the image to Cassidy and then continued. "She texted me a picture of her great-grandmother and grandmother standing next to a bed covered with the Christmas quilt. Although the picture is old and in poor condition, the image bears a strong resemblance to our quilt. Also, if you enlarge the picture, you can see the antique wardrobe we found in the playroom. I think we've found the rightful owners."

Cassidy took a moment to look at the picture. Although blurry, it was the Christmas quilt they had found hidden in the wall. "I can't believe it. Not only did you find the quilt's owner, but you also uncovered the original builders of the inn. I'd love to speak with Ms. Boothby. Do you have her contact information?"

Sarah pulled a slip of paper from her pocket. "I have her cell number and email address. I also asked if she might happen to be in the Lakeview area, but she lives near Boston. At first, she offered to drive here to meet with us, bring her documentation, and visit the inn, but with the impending storm and her grandmother in the hospital, she felt it was better to wait until after the holidays. I'll leave her number so you can call her then." Sarah headed toward the door but stopped and turned back around. "Oh, Ms. Boothby specifically mentioned how generous you are for returning the quilt. I also asked about the nativity scene, but she said neither she nor her grandmother remembered it, and it hadn't appeared in any of the old family Christmas photos."

After Sarah left her office, Cassidy looked at the old picture Ms. Boothby had sent to Sarah. It was incredible that they managed to find the rightful owner. She couldn't wait for Ms. Boothby to visit the inn.

Cassidy emailed Ms. Boothby to share her excitement about discovering the rightful owner. Considering the potential for heavy snowfall, she proposed dates after the holidays and invited Ms. Boothby to stay overnight at the inn as her guest. This would allow them to explore the inn thoroughly, dine with Sarah and a few local friends, and delve into the untold history of Crystal Lake Inn, which was previously known as the Boothby Residence.

Life truly is stranger than fiction. Cassidy had predicted they'd only have a slim chance of connecting with the quilt's original owner. Not only could she return it to the owner, but she could also receive a history lesson about the inn.

Now that she knew who the original owner was, she didn't want to wait another week or two, but the annoying weather forecast was delaying the visit. Maybe, just maybe, the storm would blow itself out to sea before reaching Boston, and Ms. Boothby could come to Lakeview next week after all. Fingers crossed.

Just as Cassidy remembered she needed to go to the playroom and search for the missing Baby Jesus, her phone rang. The call required her attention. Of course, there was a mix-up with dates for a group of friends booked for the last week of January. It would take some maneuvering to sort this out. She made a mental note to check the playroom later that day.

As Cassidy refocused on the caller, she realized that running an inn was more interesting than most people thought. Missing Baby Jesus statuettes, hidden treasures, snowstorms, budding romances, late deliveries, dirty dishes, lots of laundry, and constant cleaning…but at the end of the day, Cassidy absolutely loved owning Crystal Lake Inn.

CHAPTER TWENTY-ONE

December 21ˢᵗ

The sun shone brightly on Sunday morning, three days before Christmas Eve, although the temperature was in the low twenties. The brilliant blue sky gave a false sense that it wasn't possible for a significant snowstorm to be headed to Lakeview.

Kate woke up excited that her entire family, along with the other guests from the inn, would be attending church service together. Even Tom decided to join them. He was feeling a bit stir-crazy and thought he was up to overcoming the cumbersome crutches to attend the service.

Although the inn was closed to the public, Peter decided to serve his famous Sunday dinner, so he put the roast in the oven before they left for church. He'd marinated the meat the evening before and then placed the pan in the oven on low so it could cook slowly.

Everyone dressed up for the service, and the children wore the beautiful outfits Kate had given them. The women insisted on taking a group picture before they left for church, which sounded simple, but with so many children, it resulted in a ten-minute delay before they could leave. Luckily, the church was nearby, and they arrived with time to spare.

Entering the church, Kate shook hands with the minister and took a moment to chat with several friends from the community. Like in many churches, families had sat in the same seats for generations. Kate knew exactly where to go— she headed to the fourth row from the front, on the left side of the sanctuary. These were the same seats her family had occupied for years.

The service began, and Kate turned her attention to the front of the church. After a few announcements, the minister turned the program over to the music director, who introduced the special event of the morning. The Children's Choir was performing a unique version of "We Wish You a Merry Christmas".

Kate couldn't help but get misty-eyed when she saw her grandchildren on stage. The children wore white gowns with small aluminum foil halos on their heads. Of course, some little ones weren't singing, while others were more interested in waving to their loved ones in the pews. But overall, the program was cute and heartwarming.

After their performance, the children were ushered to another area of the church where they could have refreshments and hear an age-appropriate version of the Christmas Story.

Back in the sanctuary, Kate lost herself in memories of sitting in the same row of seats with her mother and her husband, Duncan. Grams loved attending church services with the family and was a member of the women's group.

She was renowned for her generosity and was always ready to lend a hand when needed. Kate realized that if she stayed in Lakeview, she could become more active in her church and community. She knew her mother would smile down on her with pride. This was another benefit of staying in Lakeview.

As everyone stood to sing "Silent Night," Kate reflected on the minister's message. His more modern version of the Christmas Story focused on kindness to others, humility, compassion, and the idea that miracles can happen in the most unlikely places, even in a stable. Kate thought it was a fitting ending to the service.

An hour later, the group returned to the inn, and the smell of something tasty filled the air. After quickly changing into more comfortable clothes, everyone went back to the living room, while Amanda and Cassidy headed into the kitchen to help Peter. Sarah helped serve coffee and tea to those in the living room.

Peter went into the living room to tell the group that dinner would be ready in twenty minutes.

Kate saw that the children needed something to keep them busy, so she offered to take them to the playroom, also known as Room #210, until dinner was ready.

Due to the children's varying ages, some colored while the younger ones played with blocks. Kate was once again grateful that the renovations had been finished for the CLC weeks. It was an excellent way for the children to stay busy while releasing some energy.

Kate was surprised when she realized someone else had entered the room. It was Thornton.

Some of the little ones didn't know Thornton very well, so they stayed where they were, but little Katie, who was three, walked right up to him with a children's Christmas book in her hand and said, "Uncle Thornton, please read it to me."

Since Thornton regularly visited Jack and Cassidy's house and worked with Jack on his books, Katie had gotten used to him and started calling him Uncle Thornton. The nickname stuck, so now all the children called him Uncle Thornton.

Thornton hesitated and looked at Kate for guidance. She smiled and nodded yes. He took the book from Katie and helped her settle down in front of him on a soft pillow she had brought over from the reading nook. Before he could sit back down, other children grabbed pillows and formed a small semicircle in front of the chair where Thornton had been sitting. Of course, it was a child-sized chair.

Kate's heart melted when she saw Thornton sit in the tiny chair, which was no easy feat for someone his height and age.

Opening the big picture book, Thornton began to read the story, highlighting certain characters and showing the images on each page. The children sat quietly, listening to the story of Rudolph saving Christmas. He used different voices and acted out some parts. *His years as a book publisher are paying off,* Kate thought.

The children remained attentive and quickly asked Thornton to read another book. Even though Kate could see the chair was becoming uncomfortable for him, apparently he couldn't help but say yes.

Suddenly, Kate realized what her remaining doubt was. She was a mother and grandmother, and her children, especially her little grandchildren, were incredibly important to her. Thornton had no children or grandchildren. It wasn't memories of Duncan holding her back anymore. It's whether or not Thornton and I could have a life together with this big group surrounding us. A group that will become a constant part of my life once I move to Lakeview. Until just now, I wasn't sure if he would be happy adapting to this life, with the little ones, an extended group of friends, and being physically in Lakeview.

Now she knew he was all in.

The last piece of Kate's armor broke and hit the floor. *Could this man be any sweeter? Why was she still guarding part of her heart? Maybe it's time to let it go. Just let it go.*

Downstairs, Cassidy suddenly realized she hadn't heard any noise from the children. "I just noticed it's quiet upstairs. Too quiet. Maybe we should go check if the kids have tied and gagged my mother."

Everyone in the kitchen stopped what they were doing and listened for signs of children playing upstairs.

Amanda frowned and said, "You're right. I don't hear a sound coming from the playroom."

Jennifer looked at the other women. "Addie often plays quietly in her room, but I didn't consider that there should be more noise when there is a group of little ones."

Leah, who had joined the women in the kitchen after putting her son Elijah down for his nap, said that when she dropped Ellie off in the playroom after changing her clothes, the girls had been sitting at the small table coloring in the new Christmas-themed coloring books Cassidy had bought for them. Kate was handing out crayons and stickers.

"Dinner is ready," Peter interjected. "So, it's the perfect time to gather the troops into the dining room. I'm surprised the children aren't already clamoring to eat. They usually do when we get home from church."

Cassidy, Jennifer, Amanda, and Leah decided to go to the playroom to help Kate get the children downstairs.

Cassidy slowly opened the door to the playroom. She wondered what was keeping the children so quiet and didn't want to disturb them. She was surprised to see the children sitting on pillows in front of Thornton, who had squeezed his tall frame into a child-sized chair, reading a book. He was using different voices for the various characters in the story. The little ones were captivated by him.

Kate sensed movement behind her at the edge of the partially open door. Behind Cassidy, she saw three other nervous mothers observing the touching scene, including her daughter Jennifer. The mothers looked surprised but stayed quiet. Kate winked at Jennifer, and she watched a smile slowly spread on her face.

Once Thornton finished the last words in the book he was reading, he closed it, and applause was coming from the doorway. The children decided to join in the fun and started clapping as well.

Kate noticed that Thornton had blushed slightly, but a second later, he stood up and bowed at the waist in a formal gesture.

Cassidy saved him from having to say anything else when she announced, "Dinner is ready. Please go to the sink, wash your hands, and head downstairs." Then she quickly added, "Slowly head down the stairs. Do not run."

Kate and Thornton stayed in the room to straighten things up.

After picking up the books, Kate turned to Thornton. "You were wonderful. It looks like I've been replaced as the person the children go to for reading to them. You may need to take on a part-time job as a children's book reader at the local library. All kidding aside, you did an excellent job keeping them engaged."

Thornton turned toward Kate. "Was I good enough to earn a kiss from you?"

Kate leaned into his chest, lifted her face, and kissed him. It was a quick kiss, but it put a smile on Thornton's face.

"That's the best kind of payment ever. Do I get overtime pay?" Thornton asked.

As he finished his question, he noticed that Kate's attention had been drawn to the far side of the room where a doll bed sat, full of baby dolls covered with a small quilt.

She walked over to the doll bed and reached down.

Thornton found it odd that Kate was going to pick up one of the dolls until he realized it was the Baby Jesus, missing from the cradle in the nativity scene.

Kate burst out laughing. "No wonder we couldn't find Baby Jesus. One of the children thought he belonged in the doll bed, covered by the beautiful baby quilt Sarah made for the room. I should bring him back downstairs and place him in his rightful spot. Cassidy will be relieved to know he's been found."

Looking around the area near the doll bed, Kate found another handmade quilt. It was smaller in size and covered the statuette perfectly, so she wrapped Baby Jesus in the quilt.

There. Now Baby Jesus won't be cold, and maybe whichever child brought him upstairs might be okay to leave him in the nativity scene. At least I hope so.

As they started to walk out of the room, Kate said, "Another mystery solved. Cassidy knows the identity of the antique Christmas quilt's owner, and now the missing Baby Jesus has been found. Let's hope the snowstorm blows out to sea before it reaches Lakeview, and fingers crossed, we don't have any more mysteries to solve."

She noticed Thornton giving her a perplexed look. *Well, maybe just one more,* she thought.

CHAPTER TWENTY-TWO

December 22nd

Monday morning was a quiet day at the inn. Cassidy and the other mothers took the children to the local library for a special holiday party and story time.

Kate took her time getting dressed. She brewed coffee in her room and pulled out her laptop to respond to emails and check the local weather forecast. So far, the predictions said the storm would blow out to sea north of Boston, although it seemed to be gaining strength.

After replying to several friends' holiday wishes, Kate grabbed her book, which she still hadn't finished, and sat in the cozy chair by the window. As usual, she quickly got lost in the story, blocking out everything else.

She was startled when she heard the notification sound for a text message. Picking up the phone, she saw a message from Thornton.

Thornton

> **Join me for dinner at Attillos's**

Kate

> **Love to. Time?**

Thornton

> **Leaving at six. Dress warm.**

Kate

> **OK, see you then. Thanks.**

After finishing her message, Kate wondered why Thornton reminded her to dress warmly. Of course, she would dress warmly. It was Maine, and it was winter. Was he trying to be funny?

Despite his unusual sense of humor, Kate loved Attillio's and was already planning what she would order for dinner later that day. She reminded herself to leave room for the best Tiramisu she'd ever had. Yep, save room for dessert.

Settling back into her chair with her book, she took in the view. The sunlight was so bright it was hard to believe the temperature was in the low twenties, with a forecast to fall into the low teens overnight. The snow from a few days ago still blanketed the ground. The lake shimmered with crystalline sparkles, adding to the scene's beauty outside her window.

Wanting to dive back into the book she was reading, Kate muted her phone, tucked it under the pillow on the chair, and opened the book. She didn't take long to get lost again.

A knock on her door made Kate realize she had dozed off. Looking at her watch, she saw she had been asleep for nearly an hour. That wasn't like her, but on the other hand, she'd been busy every day since arriving in Lakeview.

"Mother, it's Cassidy. Can I come in?"

Without moving from the cozy chair, Kate replied, "Yes, Cassidy. Come in."

Cassidy glanced at her mother. "Were you reading?"

"Yes, I had been reading, and then I guess I dozed off. I'm glad you knocked on my door. I need to get up and grab a light lunch."

Cassidy smiled. "That's interesting because I was just about to ask if you'd like to join me for lunch. Peter and Amanda went out shopping for a few last-minute items, but you know Peter, he left a large pot of beef stew on the stove. Care to join me for a bowl?"

Kate got up from her chair. "That sounds delicious, but just a small bowl. Thornton invited me to dinner at Attillio's tonight. I'm glad we're having an early lunch, even though I originally planned to have a small salad or sandwich. If I'm going to Attillio's, I want to save room for one of their delicious specials and the Tiramisu dessert."

Thirty minutes later, the two women rinsed the bowls from their lunch and put them in the dishwasher.

Cassidy wiped the counter and turned to Kate. "Mother, do you mind if I ask you something?"

Kate was fairly certain she knew where the conversation was headed. She'd been expecting it since she and Thornton returned from their trip to the city. "Of course, dear. What is it?"

Cassidy paused briefly. "It seems like you and Thornton are growing closer, especially since your trip. It's obvious from how he looks at you that his feelings have changed since you arrived in Lakeview, but it's hard to tell how you feel. Would you mind sharing how you're feeling? I'll understand if you're not ready to talk about it yet."

"I don't mind you asking," Kate replied. "When I first met Thornton on the train, I was still sad and feeling at loose ends. Spending time with someone I've known for decades, who knows my history and has also experienced heartbreak, made me realize that he truly understands me."

Taking a deep breath, Kate continued. "Initially, when I thought about dating again, I realized how uncomfortable it was to attend dinners with men I didn't really know and who didn't know my background. It all seemed unfathomable to me. With Thornton, it was comfortable. He is so easy to talk to and has a way of focusing solely on me, which makes me feel like he truly wants to hear what I have to say. And, the first time he kissed me, it was a sweet, innocent kiss, but I felt it all the way to my toes. It rekindled something from nearly forty years ago."

She stopped talking. Kate was trying to decide how much she wanted to share with her daughter. "I'm not sure if I ever told you this, but beyond a few of us hanging out together, and before I met your father, my feelings for Thornton went beyond just one of the group. We shared one sweet kiss, and I realized I wanted more, but he didn't respond to my overtures, and I quickly dropped it."

Cassidy asked, "Why didn't you pursue your feelings?"

"Since we arrived here, Thornton told me he had tried to tell me he had deeper feelings for me back in college, but he thought I wasn't interested. He didn't want to ruin our friendship, so I guess we both backed off."

Kate paused again to gather her thoughts and looked out toward the lake. "After all these years, I finally learned the real story. Thornton shared that he told one of my so-called friends he wanted to ask me out, but she told him I wasn't interested, and the one kiss we shared turned me off. He later discovered that she had lied because she was interested in him for herself. Looking back, the friend he mentioned had always tried to belittle Thornton to me. In hindsight, I should have realized something was off and approached Thornton myself. But then I met your father, fell in love, and the rest is history."

Looking at her daughter again, Kate said, "I can't help but think that my entire life might have been different if my friend hadn't betrayed me. However, I might not have had two beautiful daughters that I love and am so proud of, or I might not have been fortunate enough to have lived the amazing life I've experienced. Instead of dwelling on what didn't happen, I decided to focus on what might be."

Cassidy walked over to sit on the arm of her mother's chair. "Mother, I'm glad you found out about your friend—sorry, ex-friend—betraying you. Now you know that

Thornton has had feelings for you for decades. I'm so happy you're giving a deeper relationship a chance. As you know, we all love Thornton, so we're already fans. But, to be clear, I don't mean to add any pressure for you. It's your life, and you need to make your own decisions, without anyone watching your every move."

Kate leaned over and hugged her daughter. "I'm glad you understand that I need to make my own decisions. Maybe now you won't hover so much."

The two women parted ways, with Kate returning to her room.

In her quiet and cozy room, Kate reflected on everything that had happened since she returned to Lakeview. The days had been busy, but she felt more at peace than she had in a long time. Somewhere along the way, a heavy weight had been lifted from her shoulders.

Smiling to herself, she realized much of her newfound peace came from removing the last remnants of armor around her heart. Placing her rings in the jewelry box was a significant step, but even more so was admitting to herself that she was falling for Thornton. Maybe it was the first sparks of love, or perhaps it was something even more.

Right now, Kate realized she was receptive to wherever this new romantic journey might take her. She was eager to discover what Thornton had in store for tonight. With her new feelings stirring, she couldn't wait to see him.

Would she swoon the next time he kissed her? *Swoon— that old-fashioned word—why did it suddenly pop into my head? Of course, I just read it in the historical romance novel I'm reading.*

Thornton felt nervous. It was freezing outside. He hoped the extra blankets he had paid the carriage owner to put on the seat, along with the battery-operated warming blanket, would keep Kate warm during the ride to the restaurant.

Initially, he rented the horse-drawn sleigh for a round trip, but Jack suggested that a one-way trip would be more romantic. Returning home with a frozen date would probably overshadow the romantic evening he was trying to create. Thornton had agreed.

He had given careful thought to ideas for creating a romantic evening with Kate. In the summer, it was much easier. He could rent a boat for the evening with dinner included, have a picnic by the lake, or even rent a cabin on the lake with a chef to cook fresh trout. But in winter, his options were limited. When he asked Jack for suggestions, his client and friend told him that one of the most romantic evenings he and Cassidy ever had—besides their honeymoon night in a Paris hotel overlooking the Eiffel Tower—was a horse-drawn sleigh ride in the snow.

Thornton was also a little nervous because he wasn't sure how safe it was to ride in a horse-drawn sleigh to town, but the driver assured him that he never took the highway. He had a trail through the backroads that he used. The local traffic was accustomed to seeing his flashing taillights, and he assured Thornton they'd be safe.

Kate was always punctual, so Thornton knew she'd be ready at six o'clock. He arranged with Cassidy and Jack to be in the living room, blocking her view of the driveway. When the carriage arrived, he wanted them to call her to the window so she could see what was happening.

"Mother," Cassidy said. "Look outside. What's going on?"

Quickly walking to the window, Kate looked outside. As soon as Thornton realized she had seen him, he bowed and gestured toward the horse-drawn sleigh. Then he went to the front door to escort her to the romantic ride that awaited them.

By the time Kate reached the sleigh, everyone, including the children, was standing outside on the porch watching the scene. The bright flashing lights on the sleigh made it easy to see. The driver placed a stool beneath the step to the sleigh, and Thornton helped Kate get on board.

Once the passengers were settled into their seats and covered up to their necks, the driver slowly began their journey.

Kate turned to look at her host. "Thornton, what in the world were you thinking? No wonder you told me to dress warmly. I thought you had planned to walk along the decorated streets in town. It's good that I wore my fur-lined boots, puffer coat, hat, and gloves. Are you crazy?"

Thornton wrapped his arm around her shoulders and pulled her closer. "I wanted this to be a romantic evening, and a horse-drawn sleigh is about as romantic as it gets in the winter in Maine. Are you warm enough, Kate?"

"Yes. This heated blanket is fantastic, but I'm glad we're not too far from the restaurant. I don't want to get frostbite and miss my dinner. You know Attillio's is my favorite restaurant in Lakeview."

Thornton started to speak, but Kate interrupted him. "Oh no. Everyone at the restaurant will see us arrive. What will they think?"

He responded quickly. "I thought of that, too. Even though I don't mind what people think, I wanted to consider your feelings, so I asked the driver to let us off at the end of the building, which has no windows. I've also arranged for an Uber to take us back to the inn. Do these plans meet with your approval, my Lady Kate?"

Kate couldn't help but laugh. "Yes, sir. Your well-thought-out plans meet my approval. Now I can enjoy this romantic ride, the starry night, and my companion."

They arrived at the restaurant safely, although it was a bit chilly. Several people entering or leaving paused to admire the beautiful horses and the antique sleigh. Still, no one spoke, and those gathered quickly moved on, which Kate appreciated, especially since it was now completely dark and getting colder.

Mr. Artillio himself greeted Kate and Thornton at the door. "I trust you had a safe trip. We have your table ready for you. As you requested, Mr. Reed, your table is by the fireplace. You should warm up quickly."

After seating them, Mr. Artillio handed them menus and a smaller menu of tonight's specials. "I'll send your waiter over to start you off with drinks while you look at the menu. Be sure to check out tonight's specials. We have a steak and shrimp dish in white wine sauce that's getting fantastic reviews."

Thornton reached across the table and covered Kate's hand with his. "I was worried you might get uncomfortably cold on our trip here, but your hands seem to have already warmed up. Did you enjoy the ride?"

"Of course! It was wonderful. Who wouldn't enjoy something out of a fairy tale?" Kate responded.

Thornton pulled his hand back as the waiter asked for their drink orders, recommended a wine to go with the steak special, and then quickly walked away from the table.

Kate looked into Thornton's eyes. "It was a magical ride. I was shocked when I saw the sleigh waiting for me at the inn. I thought I'd be too cold, but the heated blankets and the snuggling made a cozy cocoon. Thank you for going to so much trouble. The ride will become one of my favorite memories."

"I'm so glad you enjoyed it," Thornton responded. "Now, let's decide what we want to eat and get our dinner ordered. I'm starving. I was so anxious about the arrangements going perfectly that I didn't eat lunch. I've decided on the special steak and shrimp dinner. What about you?"

Kate also thought the steak and shrimp sounded perfect.

The waiter took their order, quickly returned with freshly baked rolls, and brought their salads.

Ninety minutes later, they were drinking coffee—of course, decaf because of the late hour—and finishing the Tiramisu they had decided to share.

Kate finished the crumbs remaining on her dessert plate and set down her fork. "I'm stuffed. Everything was delicious."

A small smile played at the corners of Thornton's mouth. "Kate, I'm so glad you enjoyed the entire date. Yes, I said date. I'm hoping you agree that this is an official date. How do you feel about that?"

Hesitating briefly, Kate replied, "Yes, this is our official first date. I'm not sure how you'll ever top this one, but I'm happy to play along."

Now it was Thornton's turn to hesitate. "Kate, you have to know that my feelings for you have deepened. I'm thrilled you are finally opening up to something more serious between us. I'm not sure how all of this will work after the first of the new year, but let's not get bogged down in that discussion yet. Let's enjoy the next few weeks, celebrate the new year, and then we can see where we go from here. Is that okay with you?"

He could see Kate visibly swallowing.

"That's a lot to take in, and it feels like it's happening quickly, but in reality, it's been across four decades, so it's not like we're teenagers or starting from scratch," Kate said. "I feel fortunate to have another chance at romance, especially with someone I already know so well and admire. Thornton, you've become important to me. I know I can lean on you, trust you, and, besides, who else would go to such lengths to create such a romantic evening?"

"Kate, you've made me so happy." Thornton leaned across the table and kissed her cheek.

Thornton signaled to the waiter for the check. "If you're ready to go, I'll let our driver know, and we can get in the car. I plan to steal a few kisses in the backseat. We may be in our sixties, but I feel like a teenager again."

Kate excused herself to the ladies' room, giving Thornton time to reflect on the past few hours. He couldn't be happier with how everything had unfolded. If someone had asked him months ago whether he would reconnect with Kate, take a horse-drawn sleigh ride in the snow, and rekindle a missed chance at love, he would have laughed. But this was real. He had to admit he was head-over-heels and falling deeper with each day he spent with Kate. He couldn't wait to see what the new year would bring.

CHAPTER TWENTY-THREE

December 23ʳᵈ

Everyone woke up on Tuesday morning, excited for the next two days, despite the gathering clouds on the horizon. If they hadn't already heard about the change in forecast before coming down for breakfast, they would soon find out. It was the main topic of the day. The slate-gray skies and noticeable winds heightened the anticipation of an approaching storm.

Overnight, the meteorologists revised their forecast for Lakeview. They now predicted a major blizzard within the next twenty-four hours, most likely later that night. High winds could exceed fifty miles per hour. Snow accumulation was now measured in feet rather than inches. Widespread power outages and whiteout conditions would make travel hazardous.

True to the Mainers' tradition, they prepared for the worst. Cassidy had filled the underground propane tanks the week before, ensuring the inn could run on generator power for two weeks if necessary. The few remaining outdoor chairs and benches, which were used during the winter, had been moved to the storage building. Peter and Amanda dedicated an entire day to preparing casseroles, which were stored in the freezer in case no one could go out for dinner, making being snowed-in more enjoyable for everyone.

Additionally, Derrick and his team were on high alert. As predicted, Dr. Foster had been called to the hospital. He packed extra clothes and personal items in case he got stranded there. Peter had been kind enough to pack him a bag of homemade treats to share with others.

At breakfast, the conversation was lively, but a hint of nervousness lay beneath it.

Cassidy asked the group, "Is anyone worried about the storm? If you have any questions, please feel free to ask. While I think we've covered every blizzard-related scenario we could, we only have a few hours to make adjustments or purchases before it becomes too dangerous to go outside or into town."

Jennifer spoke up first. "I haven't experienced a Maine blizzard in years. Part of me is nervous, and the other part is excited for a white Christmas."

"I feel better about the storm knowing we're well prepared, and that we're all together," Cassidy replied. "It helps that the worst part of the storm will be overnight, so hopefully everyone can sleep through much of it."

The group discussed last-minute errands, and Cassidy and Jennier decided it would be good to get the children outside to burn off some of their energy. As the group began to part ways for their last-minute activities, Peter said, "Tonight I'm serving my minestrone soup with fresh Italian bread. Tomorrow night will be the traditional seven fishes. If you go into town, eat lightly, because I plan to serve dinner at six o'clock. You'd better be hungry. As usual, I'll probably make way too much food."

Everyone went on their way.

Marie Boothby couldn't decide what to do. The hospital called her late in the afternoon to say her grandmother's condition had slightly worsened, and they weren't allowing any visitors due to the risk of additional infections. While they still hoped she would recover from the pneumonia in a few days, her lungs were struggling, which increased her risk. For now, she was sedated and resting as comfortably as possible.

Standing in her kitchen, Marie pondered her options. She absent-mindedly wiped the stainless steel refrigerator door repeatedly. Her reflection in the refrigerator showed a young woman in her late twenties. She resembled her grandmother and was petite, with short, curly blond hair cut in a bob.

Marie's husband, Matthew, was currently deployed overseas. He often told her she reminded him of the girl next door. She had a bubbly personality, cared for others, and brought enthusiasm to everything she did.

Marie and her husband only got to talk once a week, and with her grandmother being sick and the holidays quickly approaching, she missed him more than usual.

Decisions. Decisions. Decisions. Marie knew from earlier conversations that her grandmother had expressed a strong desire to see the special Christmas quilt. Her grandmother had shared stories with Marie about the women who pieced and quilted the quilt and how the family felt sad when they realized it was lost. She hadn't been aware of the secret hiding place in the wall, but she wasn't surprised.

Also, knowing a storm was predicted, Marie listened to the local Boston forecast again. She wondered if she had enough time to quickly hop in her car, drive to Lakeview, and return the same night before the storm arrived. The stations all predicted that Boston wouldn't be hit directly before the storm moved off the coast.

Considering the pros and cons, Marie decided she should bring the Christmas quilt home to Boston in time for Christmas. Maybe it was the only thing that could help her grandmother recover from her current health crisis. She was used to driving in snow, though not in a blizzard, however, no one was calling it a 'blizzard' at that point in the Boston area.

Speaking aloud to no one but herself, Marie said, "Yes. I'm doing it. I'll leave tomorrow, pack a few things into a suitcase, add snacks and water to the car, book a hotel room for the night, and head out. I can be back early Christmas morning."

Suppose I don't tell my grandmother, my brother, or my aunts, she thought. No one would be worried anyway since their family had already decided to postpone their traditional Christmas celebration until the twenty-eighth, when her brother and his family could join them. It seemed like the perfect plan.

Marie left a message on Cassidy's phone saying she had found a room at a nearby hotel and was driving to Lakeview the next day. She planned to stop by the inn after checking out of her hotel to pick up the quilt, but would need to leave right away to get home before dark. She would schedule a future trip to Lakeview so she could spend time with Cassidy, hear more about the inn, and walk through the town, which she'd only heard stories about.

Now that she'd made her decision, Marie was overwhelmed with the need to give her grandmother the cherished quilt on Christmas night. She hurriedly left the message for Cassidy. Unfortunately, in her rush to pack and get on the road, she accidentally hit erase instead of send, and the message wasn't delivered to Cassidy's phone.

She'd gone to bed late, which caused her to get a later start to her trip than planned. After loading everything into her car, Marie left the city behind and headed north on the turnpike. Before turning on the radio to an easy listening station, she checked the local Boston news once more. The announcer said the storm would most likely bypass the Boston area, and if the storm hugged the coast, Maine might get several inches, which she knew would be plowed away by daylight the next morning. She had just enough time to get to Crystal Lake Inn, pick up the quilt, and reach her hotel room before nightfall and the storm starting.

Marie's plan would have succeeded except for three critical errors. First, she should have checked the updated weather forecast for the Lakeview area, not just Boston. Lakeview tended to get twice as much snow as Boston.

Second, Marie should have personally contacted Cassidy, who would have warned her about the impending blizzard and advised her to postpone her trip. Third, if she hadn't been eight-and-a-half months pregnant and her husband hadn't been deployed overseas for another two months, she wouldn't have been traveling alone.

Her heart was in the right place, but she seemed to be experiencing Pregnancy Brain Fog. If her husband or her family knew what she was planning, they would have found a way to stop her. It would now take a Christmas miracle for Marie's plans to work out as she expected.

CHAPTER TWENTY-FOUR

December 24th

Everyone woke up on Christmas Eve morning to a blanket of white. It was still snowing, and the winds were blowing drifts across the roads, constantly covering what the snowplows had already cleared. By first light, the snow on the walkways at the inn had been cleared, along with the parking lot, but two hours later, they were covered again.

Dr. Foster had to stay at the hospital the night before. If the snowplows were able to clear the roads, he planned to spend Christmas Eve evening with his family at the inn. If not, he knew they would be taken care of, which gave him some comfort.

Derrick and two of his staff spent the night in a small room at the police station. Most of their time was spent rescuing stranded motorists who ignored the forecast and the warnings to stay off the roads. Derrick checked in with the town maintenance manager, Mark Brooks, to confirm that the plows were out in full force, and they were. However, the secondary and back roads could take several days to fully clear. Derrick also hoped to spend Christmas Eve night with Trish at the inn.

At the inn, it was a busy hive of people trying to entertain themselves indoors. It was far too blustery to go outside. Games were set up in the living room near a roaring fire, snacks had been placed in the dining room, and Christmas tunes were playing from the overhead speakers, filling the whole inn with holiday sounds.

Peter and Amanda were baking cookies while the children decorated them. Well, there was as much icing on the children's aprons as on the cookies, but everyone was having fun, and that's what mattered most.

Kate, Cassidy, and Jennifer were wrapping the last of their gifts. They hid in Kate's room, even though they knew once the cookie decorating was finished, the little ones would soon find them.

Kate turned on the automatic coffee maker in her room and made each of them a cup of hot cocoa. It would be enough to give them a quick energy boost to finish wrapping.

Cassidy stretched. "It's been incredible to all be together for the holidays, especially with the blizzard. Yes, I said blizzard, now that the weathermen are calling the storm a blizzard. With the heavy snowfall, we're all cozy together, enjoying the holidays the way they're meant to be—shared with family and loved ones. As it turned out, I'm so glad we included Sarah, Tom, and the Foster family. And, let's not forget Thornton."

Kate wondered why her daughters both looked at her when Cassidy mentioned Thornton's name.

"Why are you two staring at me?" Kate asked.

Cassidy spoke up first, "Mother, come on and tell us what's going on. As Grams would have said, spill the beans."

Kate started to giggle, which Cassidy found adorable but so unlike her mother. Cassidy said, "Mother, you're giggling. You serve on the board of the hospital and several other nonprofits, including Duncan's former firm. I don't think the members would believe you are giggling. You're usually a well-organized, straightforward, no-nonsense person. What's gotten into you lately? Is this thing with Thornton that serious?"

Now Kate truly felt the spotlight was on her. Taking a moment to gather her thoughts, she paused and looked at her daughters. "Okay. I can't believe this is happening, but yes, I'm falling for Thornton."

Kate placed both hands over her heart and continued, "I never imagined I'd be in love again in my early sixties. It just happened. It wasn't something I ever considered, but somehow, Thornton found a small place in my heart that was open to love, and it's grown from there. The sleigh ride and romantic dinner the other evening, and watching him stuff himself into that little chair in the playroom— all contributed to sealing the deal. My resistance has been overcome."

Jennifer asked, "Have you told Thornton your feelings have changed and you're starting to fall in love with him?"

"No, not yet, but I've shared that my feelings are growing deeper. It's all happened so quickly. I don't want to ruin it by rushing into anything. Even when I tell him, I'll be clear that this fast-moving train needs to slow down so we can figure out what it truly means for us after he has to go back to the city for work in the new year."

Kate quickly added, "And I've fallen back in love with Lakeview too. I told the realtor I won't be renewing the lease on the lake house Duncan and I built a few years ago. I plan to move there in a few months. I hope you both are okay with all of this."

Worried that her daughters might be upset, Kate was happily surprised when they clapped their hands and rushed over to hug her.

After the hug ended, Cassidy said, "We're so happy for you, Mother. We already love having Thornton in our lives. We see how you light up when he's around, and he makes you happy. Jennifer and I talked about it. We are both supportive and happy for you."

The three women sat back down to finish their gift wrapping, excitedly talking about the possibility of Kate moving back to Lakeview permanently, so they could all be together.

The only cloud on the horizon was the possible issue of Thornton's job being in the city, but that was a concern for another day. Today, Kate and her daughters enjoyed their time together and prepared for the chaos of Christmas morning with five small children in the house.

Blizzard and snow-covered roads stretched outside, while warm hearts and laughter filled the inside. For just a brief moment, it was a perfect world at Crystal Lake Inn.

Later that evening, the storm pushed out of the area, but not until it had dumped almost two feet of snow on Lakeview. Fortunately, electricity was still flowing smoothly across the county, except in a few remote areas. Maine Electric Cooperative expected to restore power to all customers within a few more hours.

Lakeview resembled a Christmas card, with snow covering the streets and store awnings. The earlier wind had died down, leaving the decorative lights along Main Street free of snow and brightly illuminating the empty sidewalks.

Around ten thirty, Derrick called Trish. "Hello, sweetheart. How is everything at the inn?"

"Everything is fine here, and it's quiet. The children only agreed to go to bed around eight o'clock in anticipation of Santa coming in the morning. Most of the adults have already headed to bed, too." She quickly added, "And, Dr. Foster's replacement for the next two days was finally able to get to the hospital. Dr. Foster arrived here a few minutes ago. Peter fixed him a plate of food, and we sat with him to catch up on some of the emergencies in the Maternity Ward. Once he finished eating, he quickly went upstairs to see if Leah was still awake or if she needed help with anything. He's hoping to spend the next two days with us at the inn."

"I feel better now that everyone is at the inn together and not out on the roads," Derrick said. "The road between town and the inn is almost clear, but so much snow has been piled up along the edges of the road that it's dangerous on some of the winding backroads. The maintenance crews are working around the clock, but until the winds recently died down, it was almost impossible to keep the surfaces they'd already plowed clear."

Trish spoke to him now in a sultry voice. "Everyone is safely tucked into the inn except for you, darling. Can't you come home now before you get any more emergency calls? I can't wait for you to get here. When do you think you'll be home? I want to wait up for you and…"

Derrick chuckled, picturing his impish wife in a negligee, her blond hair gleaming in the moonlight, her blue eyes smoldering, although in reality, she probably had on a set of those silly holiday-themed pajamas. "I wish I could come home now, but I can't leave for an hour or so. I'm waiting for the deputies to report in after their last rounds at eleven, file their reports, and head home. Then I'll be able to join you. Since the inn is only about two miles from the station, it should be an easy drive. Expect me around midnight, but you don't have to wait up."

"I might go upstairs to our room, but I plan to stay awake so I can be the first to wish you a very Merry Christmas. Be safe, and I'll see you soon."

The couple hung up. Derrick hoped he could keep his promise to be home soon. In his line of work, anything could happen, and it often did.

It was almost midnight when the deputies finished their final check-ins and filed their reports. Derrick was the last to leave the station. He quickly turned off the lights and stuffed his tall, muscular frame into this patrol car. He didn't even leave the parking lot before his phone rang. Thinking it was probably Trish checking in, he was alarmed when he saw that the local emergency number was transferring a call to his cell phone.

Putting his car in park, he picked up his phone and identified himself. The caller was a resident who had just left the late church service. They'd seen skid marks off the side of the road leading from town toward the inn. They had stopped but didn't see any vehicles off the road. They assumed whoever had skidded had regained control and continued on their way. However, with the freezing weather and heavy snowfall, they didn't feel comfortable not notifying the local police. Derrick thanked the caller and said he would investigate since he was already heading in that direction.

Driving slowly along the road to the inn, Derrick didn't notice any skid marks. He hoped the caller was correct and the car had managed to get back on the road. Still moving slowly and shining his large outside light along the snowbanks, he was less than a mile from the inn when he noticed a long set of skid marks leading off the road and directly into a big pile of snow.

Derrick pulled his car as far off the road as he could without getting stuck, then turned on the flashing lights on top of his police vehicle. He stepped out with his flashing lantern and followed the length of the skid marks. At first, he didn't see any vehicles, but there was a five-foot wall of plowed snow blocking his view.

Although he'd never been convinced that people in his line of work had a special intuition, he chose not to ignore the strange sensation telling him to climb over the snowbank. When he reached the top, the snow pile gave way, and he slid back down. For a second, he thought he'd seen the tiny flash of red taillights.

His heart rate quickly increased as he climbed out of the huge drift of powder, certain the lights had been there. He knew he couldn't easily reach the car due to the shifting snow. Derrick was fairly sure the lights were taillights of a smaller model car. How long had the car been stranded? Was anyone still inside?

Derrick brushed the snow off his uniform and coat and quickly assessed the situation. He knew that without a shovel to help him get over the snowbank, he would be wasting valuable time, so he returned to his patrol unit to get one he had stored in his trunk. Then he called the emergency line to report the incident. He noted that he was on-site but hadn't yet reached the vehicle. As soon as he could provide an update or if the EMTs were needed, he'd call them back. His first priority was to see if anyone was still inside the car.

Grabbing the shovel, Derrick hurried back to the car. Shoveling as quickly as he could, he reached the driver's side door. Shining his flashlight into the window, he was startled to see a person wrapped in several blankets and a knitted hat, which almost covered their face. He couldn't tell if the person was male or female.

The figure remained still, prompting him to tap on the window several times. At first, he feared the worst, but thankfully, the driver began to move and then shifted in their seat toward the window. He signaled for the driver to lower the window.

Derrick identified himself and asked if the occupant was okay and how long they had been stranded. That's when he realized it was a woman, a young woman who sounded scared.

The driver said she had been there for several hours but had been able to start the car periodically to use the heater. Luckily, she had several blankets and extra clothes in the car to help keep her warm, but she was down to a quarter tank of gas and worried she would freeze before anyone found her.

Derrick told her to stay covered up. He asked if she was hurt, and she said no. While he couldn't dig her car out of the snowbank, he could clear the snow from her door and make a path to his patrol car, which he'd left running. It would be warm inside.

Before she rolled her window back up, Derrick asked her if she lived nearby and where she was headed. She said she was from Boston and going to the hotel on the other side of town, but the hotel had called her earlier to say their power was out and they didn't have a generator, so they were closing until after Christmas. She thought she'd find somewhere else to stay, but then the storm and wind worsened, and she skidded into a snowbank. Of course, her phone died, and she didn't want to risk draining the car's battery by charging it.

Derrick asked the driver again if she was hurt or needed the EMTs. She said no. He told her he needed to go back to his car to update the dispatcher and tell them the EMTs weren't necessary and that he'd add her vehicle to the long list of those needing a tow in the morning—then he'd be right back. He told her to keep her window rolled up until he returned.

Knowing that everything was fully booked or closed, his only option was to take the woman back to the police station and let her stay in the small room he had used the night before, but if he did that, he'd also have to stay at the station. It was a policy they strictly enforced.

He quickly reviewed his options and found only one viable choice, then promptly called Trish.

No waiting for phone pleasantries, as soon as the call connected, Derrick said, "We've got a problem."

Trish immediately cut him off, worried he was hurt. He assured her he was okay and quickly explained what happened.

Needing to get back to the driver, he laid out the issue. "Trish, there are no safe places nearby for her to stay tonight. Even if I could get a tow truck here quickly—which I doubt—I wouldn't leave her alone. If I take her to the police station, I'd have to stay with her, but more than that, I can't bear to put her in that small room on a cot on Christmas morning. Is there any way we could let her spend the night at the inn?"

Trish hesitated, "In the morning, it will be chaos here. The families will be celebrating Christmas, and the kids and gifts will be everywhere. It's not the best time to have a stranger join us, but you're right. We can't just put her in the awful bunk room. Please remind me to share my ideas for making it a bit nicer. Anyway, back to the issue, Cassidy would shudder if I told you there's no room at the inn and we turned someone away, especially at Christmas. Okay, bring her here, but please explain the situation at the inn so she's not caught off guard in the morning."

Derrick softly said, "Now I know why I love you so much. You always find a way to help others. Expect us in fifteen minutes. I need to finish shoveling the snow away from her door so I can get her out of the car. See you soon. And, thank you again. Now, I can be her hero."

Returning to the car, Derrick quickly cleared the snow from the door. He tried to open it, but had to keep shoveling more snow away. Finally, he was able to open the door.

He explained he had secured a room for her at a nearby inn less than a mile away. He continued to say that the inn was officially closed to the public for the holidays, but he had connections there, and they were happy to help under these circumstances. He also mentioned that he, his wife, and other family and friends were staying at the inn for the holidays.

The driver hesitated about what to do, but realizing she had no other options, she thanked him and began gathering her belongings. He saw a suitcase in the back seat, opened the door, and took it out.

Derrick warned the woman, "Be careful when you get out. There's still a lot of snow, but I've made a path over the snowbank to my police car. Here, let me take your hand and help you out. By the way, my name is Derrick, the Chief of Police. Can I ask what your name is?"

Hesitantly, she responded, "My name is Marie." The young woman seemed to struggle getting out of the car. At first, Derrick was worried she was hurt, but as soon as he helped her out of the car and she stood up, he was shocked to see that she was pregnant. From his estimate, she was very pregnant.

"Are you sure you're okay?" Derricked asked.

Marie smiled, "I guess you noticed that I'm pregnant. About eight-and-a-half months pregnant, to be exact. I feel fine. No pains or anything like that, but thanks for your concern."

Derrick knew a well-qualified prenatal specialist was staying at the inn, so he decided to stop asking questions for now. He carefully helped her into his car.

Not wanting Derrick to realize how utterly foolish she had been—causing this risky trip because of her failed attempts at proper planning—Marie stuck to the basic facts about why she was out in a blizzard. She told him she was heading to the hotel and had a very important present to pick up. She quickly changed the subject by telling Derrick how grateful she was that he had found her.

When the two arrived at the inn, Derrick unlocked the front door and helped Marie out of her coat. Before he could show her into the living room, Marie quickly asked to use the powder room she saw off the lobby. He told her he'd meet her in the living room just down the hallway.

Derrick moved into the living room, where he was surprised to see a blazing fire, two cups of hot cocoa, and two sandwiches on the coffee table.

Trish had been waiting for them, and when she heard his tires crunching on the snow, she placed their refreshments on the table and stoked the fire.

When Derrick entered the room, he quickly went to his wife, hugged her, and kissed her on the cheek. He also whispered in her ear, "Don't act surprised, I didn't know she was pregnant until after she got out of the car."

Trish pulled away from the hug. "What?"

Before Derrick could say anything else, Marie walked into the room. The first thing she saw was the hot cocoa and the sandwich. "Wow, this is more than I expected. I had eaten all my snacks and was starting to get hungry. Is one of those sandwiches for me?"

Trish moved closer to the unexpected visitor, picked up the plate, and handed it to her guest. "Yes, I thought you might be hungry, but I didn't know what you would like to eat this late at night, so I figured a sandwich might be a good option. I can get you something warm. We have minestrone soup I can heat if you'd prefer."

Marie said the sandwich was perfect.

"By the way, I'm Derrick's wife, Trish. It seems he's lost his manners. Please sit down and enjoy your sandwich and cocoa."

Marie sat down and smiled at Trish and Derrick. "I can't tell you how thankful I am for Chief Williams coming to my rescue. I can't imagine what would have happened if I had stayed there all night and had run out of gas. But I prefer not to think about it. By the way, my name is Marie."

Stifling a yawn, Marie apologized to her hosts.

Trish realized the young woman must be exhausted. "We can chat in the morning. First, you need a good night's sleep. I'm sorry we don't have better accommodations for you. The inn is fully booked. Luckily, we have a brand-new twin bed in the playroom that has never been slept on, with fresh linens. The room comes with an en-suite bathroom that includes clean towels and toiletries. I think Derrick explained the chaos we'll have in the morning. By the way, beverages and Danish will be available in the dining room starting at six for those who need to get up early with children, and a full breakfast will be served at eight. Feel free to sleep late or join us for breakfast."

Placing her empty plate on the tray, Marie turned toward Trish. "Thank you for everything and for letting me interrupt your holiday," she said, tears in her eyes. "I'm so exhausted, I'd be happy to sleep on the sofa, but an actual bed sounds wonderful. I don't want to intrude on your Christmas celebration, so I'll stay in my room until breakfast time."

"Don't be silly," Trish said. "We'd love to have you join us. You can come down whenever you're feeling up to it, and we'll see what we can do to get your car towed here. Maybe then you can get on your way and not interfere with your holiday plans any further. There must be a fascinating story behind why you were out on such a terrible night, but all that can wait until tomorrow."

Trish and Derrick turned off the lights, put out the fire, and walked Marie upstairs to the playroom. Once they had her settled, they went to their room.

Derrick raised his hand, expecting a flood of questions from his wife. "As I said, I don't know more than what I already told you. Marie said she made some stupid mistakes in planning her trip, her hotel shut down, and then she skidded off the road. The rest you know. I'm also exhausted and want to get into bed and cuddle up with my wife. I desperately need a few hours of sleep before the inn erupts with children, adults, laughter, and chaos."

Trish knew he was right. They both needed to get some sleep. In the morning, they could review everything and try to help Marie reach her destination. She kissed her husband and turned off the light.

Within minutes, Trish was asleep, but Derrick couldn't quiet his mind. He kept thinking about what could have happened if he hadn't investigated the skid marks. He was good at his job because he paid close attention to details, but on a cold night around midnight, all he'd wanted to do was get home and hug his wife. He was glad he'd listened to his instincts over his desires.

He thought back to when he saw the skid marks and checked the area along the road, and didn't initially find anything. What had made him look further? He was surprised when he realized it was more than just a policeman's instinct. Maybe, just maybe, on a special night, someone was watching over him and Marie, and that made him reexamine the area around the curvy part of the road.

He was still stunned when he thought about seeing the taillights. There wasn't an easy answer for what had pushed him earlier tonight, but whatever, or whoever, it was, he was extremely grateful.

Taking a few deep breaths in and out, he finally calmed down. As he fell asleep, he said a prayer and thanked the good Lord for allowing him to help a pregnant woman find room at the inn on Christmas Eve.

CHAPTER TWENTY-FIVE

December 25th

Kate woke up around three o'clock, sensing that something had awakened her. She stayed in bed, listening for any sounds. She hoped none of the children were already awake, eager to go downstairs. After waiting a few minutes and hearing nothing, she settled back down and pulled the quilt up to her chin. The room wasn't cold, but she was certain something had woken her. It left her feeling a little on edge.

A few minutes later, Kate heard the noise again. It sounded like footsteps walking back and forth across one of the rooms. She decided to find out where the noise was coming from. She put on her robe and slippers and quietly slipped out her bedroom door.

The rooms next to hers were quiet. She decided to walk to the end of the hall, and if she didn't hear anything, she'd go back to bed. Maybe it was one of the little ones needing a hug from their mother or a glass of water.

As she approached Room #210, she heard a sound like the whining of a small kitten. Oh no, one of the children must have brought in a stray cat. Now she knew she needed to investigate further.

She pressed her ear against the door to better hear the noise. If it was a small animal, she'd be careful not to scare it, or it might hide where she couldn't find it. Then she remembered that she had some cheese in her room, so she went back, cut two small pieces, and placed them on a plate. She added a little milk to a bowl. Now she felt more prepared for what she thought she'd find once she opened the door.

Walking back down the hall, Kate paused outside Room #210. She didn't hear anything, so she slowly opened the door. The room was dark except for a faint light shining under the bathroom door. She was shocked when the light barely illuminated the silhouette of a woman sitting on the tiny single bed. *OMG!* What was going on? Who was this woman? How did she get into the inn?

Before Kate could start asking her questions, she quickly realized the person in the room was a woman who appeared to be in labor! Kate hurried over to the woman, but she still had the plate of cheese and the bowl of milk in her hands. She quickly set them on the nearby table and reached over to turn on the bedside lamp.

Kate softly said, "Hi, I'm Kate. I'm staying at the inn. I don't know who you are or when you joined us, but you seem to be in pain. Are you in labor? Can I help in any way?"

The woman, sitting on the edge of the bed, crouched over and spoke softly, "I'm Marie. It's a long story, but my car went off the road, my phone died, and the hotel where

I was supposed to stay closed because of the storm. Chief Williams found me, and Trish kindly offered for me to stay at the inn. I'm not due for another two weeks, but I think nature has other plans for tonight. Yes…I'm in labor."

Marie winced in pain as a contraction wracked her body, then she took a few deep breaths until the wave subsided. "About two hours ago, the contractions were sporadic and far apart, so I went back to sleep. I was exhausted. Then, I had to get up to go to the bathroom, and my water broke. Now, the contractions are only five minutes apart. This is my first baby, and I know from the childbirth classes I took that I need to get to the hospital. I was trying not to wake anyone up. I've already been a bother tonight."

"I don't want to overstep," Kate said softly, "but I think we have a problem. The roads between here and the hospital were cleared, but are now icy. I'm not sure how long it will take the EMTs to arrive and then transport you to the hospital. I need to get some help. I promise, I'll be right back. Try to relax."

Before Kate could leave the room, Trish was at the door, wearing holiday-themed pajamas and wiping sleep from her eyes. "Is something wrong?" she asked.

Opening the door wider to let Trish inside, Kate explained the situation, and Trish said she was aware Derrick had rescued Marie and brought her to the inn.

Trish quickly walked over to Marie. "Oh no. Let me think for a minute."

Marie asked for a glass of water. Trish went to the bathroom to get it.

Kate walked back over and took Marie's hand. "Don't worry, we'll figure this out. There are four women in this inn tonight who've had babies. Between us, I'm sure we can help you with what nature and your body already know how to do." Marie was clinging to Kate's hand, not letting go.

At this point, Kate didn't know that Dr. Foster had returned to the inn and was just down the hall.

Coming out of the bathroom, Trish handed the glass to Marie and crouched down to be at her eye level. "These may not be the circumstances you dreamed of for bringing this baby into the world, but luckily, we have a good backup team on-site. My husband and I have delivered a baby in an emergency before, although it was in the backseat of a police car, so if it comes to that, we could help. But fortunately, we have a much better option. Dr. Foster, the local neonatal doctor and head of the neonatal unit at Lakeview Hospital, is staying with us. He's just down the hall."

Kate said, "Oh, I wasn't aware he had been able to get back to the inn last night. That's fantastic news. I'll stay here with Marie if you'll run and get Dr. Foster. I'm sure he'll understand the interruption when you explain the situation."

Before they could exit the room, there was a knock on the door. Kate quickly opened it and found Dr. Foster standing there with his doctor's bag held tightly in his hand.

Looking up in surprise, Kate said, "How did you know we needed you?"

"It seems doctors have a sixth sense when someone is in labor, so here I am. I also heard the unmistakable sounds of a woman in labor, and, confused about why I would hear that in this house tonight, I decided to grab my bag and follow the sounds, which brought me here."

He walked over to Marie and introduced himself. He asked her about her due date, her contractions, and any issues she had experienced during her pregnancy. He also asked if there was someone she wanted them to call on her behalf.

Marie started to cry softly. Between sobs, she explained that her husband was deployed overseas and wasn't allowed to come home. She expected him in two months, but he'd miss this important event. The doctor handed her a tissue and said they'd try to reach him with good news when they had the chance. Marie gave them his cell number, but mentioned he was out on a training mission and they weren't allowed to answer their phones. She did have a number to call in case of emergencies. They'd ask Derrick to make the call since he'd know better how to navigate the military bureaucracy.

Dr. Foster turned to Kate and Trish. "If you ladies will excuse me, I need to examine this young lady to figure out how much time we have or don't have. In the meantime, Trish, can you ask Derrick to check on the timing for an ambulance and EMTs to arrive? Give me five minutes with Marie, and you can come back in."

Marie looked up at the doctor and asked, "Would it be okay if Kate stayed? My mother passed away a few years ago, and Kate reminds me of her. She was so calm earlier. I think it would help me not to panic. Kate, would you mind staying with me?"

Kate looked at Dr. Foster, who said, "That would be fine. Anything to help you through this is considered good medicine by me."

Trish slipped out the door and headed to their room. Derrick had heard the commotion and was already getting dressed. "What's going on around here tonight? It sounds like Santa came down the chimney early this Christmas."

"Well... it's not Santa, but it might be the Stork," Trish said, trying not to laugh. "A baby will be born at the inn tonight. Thank goodness it's not in the backseat of your police car again. Fortunately, Dr. Foster arrived earlier and is examining Marie. He asked if you could contact the EMTs to see if they can even get here and if they can, how quickly."

Derrick, who usually wasn't surprised by any medical emergency, still looked stunned. "Okay, let me call dispatch, but right before I went off my shift, the EMTs were called back to their station due to the hazardous road conditions. Reports indicated that the roads between here and the hospital aren't passable. The snow had blown back over the ice-covered roads, especially between here and the hospital."

Trish waited while Derrick made a few quick phone calls.

When Derrick hung up, he turned to his wife. "It's not good. There was already an emergency, and the EMTs made it to the hospital, but just barely. The primary road from town to the hospital was a sheet of ice. Mark Brooks was contacted to get a sand truck out there, and they will head this way as soon as possible. It will be at least a few hours before the EMTs can arrive. Let me go speak with Dr. Foster."

Trish followed Derrick back to Room #210. He gently knocked on the door. Kate walked over to see who it was, and when she saw Derrick, she stepped back to let him in.

Derrick smiled at Marie, and like everyone else, he said, "Don't worry, you're in excellent hands." Then he turned toward the doctor. They spoke briefly, but before they could finish their conversation, Marie experienced another contraction, the second in the past five minutes.

Taking full command of the situation, Dr. Foster announced, "Well, folks, it seems this little one is ready to come into the world. We don't have time to wait for the EMTs. Thankfully, I've delivered hundreds of babies, many in less hospitable places."

The Doctor explained what he needed. He wasn't shy about giving orders, telling individuals what to do, and asking Kate to go into the bathroom to thoroughly wash her hands and grab a paper gown from his bag. It seemed the doctor was well prepared for anything.

Kate was momentarily stunned. "What?"

Dr. Foster told her, "Now that we need to deliver the baby here, I was hoping you would stay to support Marie. You seem to help her relax and focus on her breathing. Everyone else is busy gathering the other supplies I need, and I want Derrick here since he's attended many emergency procedures over the years, and I know he will stay calm. Is that okay with you?"

Kate felt herself tearing up and leaned down to speak directly to Marie. "Of course, I'll stay with you. I'd be honored."

Everyone sprang into action as another contraction shook Marie's petite body. Dr. Foster declared it was show time. Fortunately, since the playroom had recently been renovated, there were freshly laundered blankets, and they found a box of newborn diapers and the perfect-sized onesie in the girls' baby doll diaper bag.

Not even two hours later, the sound of a crying baby echoed through the inn. It was after five in the morning, and most of the adults were already downstairs, sipping the strong coffee Peter had prepared for them.

Surprisingly, the children slept peacefully through the whole event. When the baby's first cries were heard downstairs, the adults quietly cheered and prayed for the mother and newborn's good health.

Cassidy heard the noise and came rushing downstairs. It seemed that Trish and Kate had decided not to wake Cassidy when the emergency with Marie started. Everything was under control, and Cassidy had a long day ahead of her.

Trish had just started to explain the situation to Cassidy, but only got as far as Derrick's rescue, someone going into labor, and Dr. Foster delivering a baby, when Trish noticed Kate coming down the stairs in her rumpled pajamas.

Kate looked tired but happy. "It's a boy—a healthy baby boy, weighing over seven pounds on the bathroom scales! Mother and baby are doing fine. The doctor is currently preparing them for transport to the hospital. Derrick heard from the EMTs, and they'll be here soon. The sand truck was able to get to the roads out our way, making way for the emergency vehicles to get to the inn. It doesn't look like there will be time to visit them before they leave the inn. I'm going to clean up and go back into her room."

Turning to leave the room, Kate suddenly stopped and said, "Oh, the baby still doesn't have a name. Please don't ask the mother the name of her baby. She'll cry because she and her husband were supposed to agree on a name during their weekly call, but that was before he was sent on a last-minute military training mission overseas. When the doctor asked her for the baby's name, she burst into tears. For now, he's just our Christmas miracle."

Heading for the stairs, Kate stopped once again and added, "Marie said that I reminded her of her mother, and she asked me to stay close by. WOW! It seems I now have another grandchild, well... sort of." She brushed away a tear, smiling, and finally went upstairs.

The ambulance and EMTs arrived before six a.m., and Marie and her son were safely loaded and on their way to Lakeview Hospital. Dr. Foster briefly stopped in the lobby to kiss his wife and apologize for missing another Christmas morning with her and the children. Leah said she knew what she was getting into when she married him. He said he would be back in a few hours and not to make the children wait to open their gifts.

As he walked out the door, Leah smiled, waved, and told herself there would likely be another emergency, and if they were lucky, he might make it back in time to join them for dinner. Such was the life of a doctor.

By seven o'clock, all the children were awake and rushing downstairs. It sounded like a herd of elephants. It took only five minutes for the area around the tree to become completely chaotic, with boxes, wrapping paper, and toys scattered everywhere.

Always prepared, Cassidy casually pulled out a bag of various-sized batteries. After inserting them into the toys, the noise level increased, but the children's excitement overshadowed concerns about the volume.

Kate realized it was exactly what Cassidy had dreamed of for their Crystal Lake Christmas. She walked over to Thornton, who had wisely taken a seat away from the tree. "So, now you know how hectic it is when my entire crew gets together. My family and close friends have grown over the years, and I expect it will continue to expand. You can see how crazy our holidays can get. And it seems there are always unexpected surprises. If you want to run away, now would be the time."

Thornton looked around the room, grinning. "It's perfect. I guess I never knew what I was missing, but if this is special to you, it's special to me, too." Without worrying about all the eyes in the room, he reached over, pulled Kate closer to him, wrapped her in an embrace, and placed a passionate kiss on her lips. Everyone was so busy opening gifts and playing with new toys, they hardly noticed.

A call came for Kate. It was Dr. Foster who said he had someone on the line who wanted to speak to her. "Kate, it's me, Marie. I didn't get the chance to properly thank you for your kindness this morning. As you know, my mother passed away, so it's just me, my husband, my brother, and my grandmother. I miss all of them, especially now, but you were right there the entire time, holding my hand and saying soothing and encouraging words. I hope we get the opportunity to get better acquainted. Even though we aren't related by blood, you'll always hold a special place in my heart."

Marie continued, "Please tell everyone that my husband surprised me. He wasn't on a mission, but was flying home to be with me. I guess I'm the one who surprised him in the end. He's on his way here now from Boston. Dr. Foster said the baby and I are fine, and we can go home later today. My husband should be here any minute—that's why I wanted to call you now, before I leave."

It took Kate a moment to catch up with Marie's story. "I'm so glad I could be there for you. I've said a thank you prayer for Derrick finding you and for Dr. Foster staying with us at the inn. It seems the universe was aligning things for the event, even when we had no idea a Christmas baby would be born. I'm still a little confused about how your husband knew where you were."

"That's another fortunate set of circumstances," Marie responded. "When he didn't find me at home, he went to my grandmother's house. Luckily, a neighbor saw him knocking on the door repeatedly and told him she was in the hospital. Fortunately, she's doing much better. We got on a video call, and I told her about our precious little boy. After she set me straight about the antics I had pulled, she cried and sent thanks to everyone who helped me."

Marie sniffed back tears. "When it's safe for us to travel, I want to return to the inn so we can say a proper thank you. Finding such wonderful and caring friends, in the middle of a blizzard on Christmas, is like the shining star on top of the tree."

Kate also had tears in her eyes. "I feel the same way. Cassidy said there will always be room for you and your family at Crystal Lake Inn."

There was silence on the line, and Kate wondered if the connection had dropped. "Marie, are you still there?"

"Yes, I'm still here. Kate, did you say Crystal Lake Inn?"

Kate thought it was an odd question, "Yes. Crystal Lake Inn. Why do you sound surprised?"

Marie started to laugh, "Through all of this, no one specifically said I was at the Crystal Lake Inn. I was so out of it by the time Derrick drove me there, and it was pitch dark. I didn't see the sign, and no one mentioned anything other than calling it the inn."

Now Kate was thoroughly confused. "I'm not sure why the name of the inn is so important at this point?"

"Kate, I'm Marie Boothby, the great-granddaughter of the original quilter of the Christmas quilt your daughter found behind the wall. I didn't actually meet Cassidy or Sarah last night. They were the only two who knew my name and connection to the Christmas quilt, and I only linked their names to the Crystal Lake Inn. I don't know if anyone else staying at the inn knew my last name besides Derrick and Dr. Foster. I didn't connect the dots. Again, I wasn't thinking clearly. And by then, the quilt wasn't top of mind for me or anyone else at the inn, I'm sure!"

Kate glanced across the room at the gathered group, who had noticed the tears in her eyes and grew worried. They now watched her to see who the caller was and why she went from looking happy to sad and then surprised all within a few minutes.

Kate turned away from the group so they wouldn't hear the rest of the conversation. Something exciting just happened, and she meant to keep it to herself a little longer. "I guess we have a lot more to discuss, but that can all wait until your husband arrives and you are safely back at home in Boston," she told Marie. "Call if you need anything while you're still at the hospital, or if you need a place to stay tonight. If not, promise to call me next week so we can all hop on a video call and do proper introductions. It seems there are more surprises to discuss than your little bundle of joy."

Kate turned around after hanging up and saw everyone silently staring at her, waiting for her to explain the conversation she had just had.

"So that was our happy momma calling to say her husband surprised her by coming home to the US and is on his way to the hospital." With that, Kate quickly walked over and sat in the middle of the chaos with the children, teary-eyed but smiling. She'd eventually share the secret of the link between Marie and the beautiful Christmas quilt, but for now, she was too emotional with everything that had transpired over the past few hours to give the news calmly.

The rest of the adults turned their attention back to the children and the lively celebration.

Thornton was sitting on the couch and leaned over to Kate, who was seated at his feet on the floor. Tenderly, he turned her face to his and whispered, "Hmmm, you seem like you might have more to share, my lovely Kate...I can take one look at you and know you're hiding something."

Kate smiled and pulled him down to sit beside her on the floor, "Yes. The secret is that I'm in love with you. I love you, Thornton Reed." She could tell he was about to pull her into an embrace in the middle of the chaos, so she gently pushed him away.

Unexpectedly, Thornton lost his balance and fell into a pile of empty boxes. The children thought he was playing a game and started to join in the fun. When Thornton tried to straighten himself and go back to Kate to confess his love, the children had him pinned down, so he silently mouthed the words, "I love you too."

Kate understood what he was trying to tell her, and it warmed her heart. This was the season for special blessings and surprises. She was fortunate to have her family and friends all together, to witness the miracle of birth, participate in Christmas traditions, and "hear" that Thornton loved her. Maybe even more surprising was realizing she loved him, too. Her heart had room for many more feelings than she had ever imagined.

As she got up and walked over to the window to look out at the snow-covered lake, it suddenly hit her. When there was no room at the inn for Mary and Joseph, they found shelter. The Baby Jesus was born in a stable, wrapped in swaddling clothes, and placed in a manger because there wasn't room at the inn. Last night, with no room at the original hotel, they found a room at the inn for Marie, where her baby was born in a playroom, swaddled in a blanket, and placed in a doll's cradle.

Kate's last thought as she stepped away from the window to join the people most important in her life was that there should always be room at the inn, your home, or in your heart.

In their tiny piece of paradise known as Crystal Lake Inn, what happened last night was truly a Christmas miracle.

EPILOGUE

Kate sat on the front porch of Crystal Lake Inn in her favorite rocking chair, enjoying a beautiful spring day. Over the past few weeks, the trees had turned a bright green as tiny leaves burst open, promising to be full and vibrant soon. Unlike in other parts of the country, spring still carried the risk of overnight freezing temperatures in Lakeview, Maine, but the last two weeks had warmed up considerably. Today was the most beautiful day yet.

The landscaping around the inn was also in its early blooming stage, but you could already see tiny buds forming as the sun seemed to direct its rays toward each little plant. After a brief shower overnight, you could smell the sweetness of the honeysuckle and lilac plants.

"Mother," Cassidy said as she stepped onto the porch with two steaming mugs. "I thought you might be ready for a mid-morning cup of coffee."

Kate turned her head toward the chair next to her, where Cassidy sat down, and placed the mugs on the small table between their rocking chairs.

"Oh, you startled me. I guess I was lost in thought," Kate said.

"Are you okay? Is something wrong?"

Thinking about everything on her mind, Kate decided it was time to be honest with her daughter. She had been waiting until Jennifer and her family returned to Lakeview—where they'd moved to in the New Year—from a trip to Disney World during their school's spring break to share the news, but she didn't want Cassidy to worry unnecessarily.

"There's nothing wrong," Kate began, "but I've been deep in thought about several topics. Let me share the big news with you first. Thornton asked me to marry him last weekend when we were in the city."

Before Kate could finish her thought, Cassidy jumped up, ran to her mother, and hugged her tightly. "I'm so happy for you, but wait—I don't see a ring on your finger. You did say yes, didn't you?"

Kate smiled and said, "Of course, I said yes. But Thornton wanted to talk to you and Jennifer before he proposed. He tried to get your permission, not because he needed it, but because it was important to him, and he knew it meant a lot to me. You and your sister haven't been in the same place at the same time for weeks. Between you joining Jack on his book tour and Jennifer getting her family settled into their new home, he hasn't been able to connect."

After hugging her mother, Cassidy eagerly asked, "Mother, was it a romantic setting? How did he propose?"

"He hadn't originally planned to propose when he did, but it was a romantic night at our favorite Italian bistro. The violin player had just walked away from our table, and Thornton had this serious look on his face. He suddenly took my hand, said he needed me in his life, loved me deeply, and asked me to marry him. He said it felt like the perfect time. We're picking up the rings next week. I was supposed to keep it a secret until he could speak with you and Jennifer, but it seems I can't manage to keep a secret. I'll call Jennifer today and tell her myself, so please keep it quiet a little longer."

Cassidy sat back down. "That's so exciting, Mother. That's happy news, but I feel there is something else bothering you."

"You know me too well," Kate replied. "Thornton and I started discussing wedding plans, and we both agreed. We want to have it here, at the inn. Just something small with family and a few of our closest friends, some of whom are from the city. To host the out-of-town guests, we'd need to take over the entire inn. We understand that would be inconvenient and would result in a loss of revenue, but we're happy to cover it."

"I'd love to host your wedding here," Cassidy said excitedly. "It's not inconvenient, but I'm already fully booked through summer and most of fall. When are you planning to get married?"

Smiling at her daughter, Kate replied, "How about Christmas? You already plan to close the inn for the last two weeks of the year and are organizing another Crystal Lake Christmas event. Could you also add a wedding to CLC? I know it's a lot to ask."

Cassidy looked momentarily stunned. "That might actually work. Yes, I'd love to host your wedding and guests. Now that I think about it, it's the perfect time for your wedding. Besides, what's a little more chaos during the most hectic time of the year?"

Suddenly, Cassidy's phone rang. She told Kate it was a call she needed to take from her office, so she left her mother on the porch but promised to return with her notebook. "Don't you dare leave this porch until I can start to create my list of things we need to do. As always, I plan to have every detail in a spreadsheet. I can't wait until you tell Jennifer. Then we can both drill you with questions. I've got to run. I'll be back in a few minutes."

Once Kate was alone again, she picked up her coffee and took a few sips. She noticed a bit of caramel had been added. That was her favorite—it added a hint of sweetness to her black coffee.

A lot had changed over the past few months. The relationship between her and Thornton had grown closer. While he often spent time in the city, he was frequently in Lakeview for several days each month and nearly every weekend. He had become a regular on the train and used the travel time to finish any urgent work, so their weekends could be just for them.

Kate was surprised when Thornton announced to the board of Patterson Publishing that he planned to retire at the end of the year. She was even more amazed when he said he wanted to move to Lakeview. They could build a new house or add an extension to her current lake house. Their family kept expanding, and they needed more space. He wanted to keep his condo in the city for the foreseeable future, and it would be a good place for them to stay when they returned to see plays and visit friends.

She thought about how her circle of family and friends had grown.

Jennifer and her family had settled into the Lakeview community once they'd moved from Europe, and Addie was thriving in her school and with her dance training at the local studio. Michael continued to travel to Europe every few months, but so far, he had typically been gone only for a week or two per trip. Jennifer was helping out at the inn and working part-time at Crystal Lake Gifts.

Tom's broken leg healed, and Sarah was preparing for the busy summer months at the Artisans Market on the mountain. It had continued to grow, just like Tom's electrical business. One of the first things Tom did after his cast was removed was to expand the powder room on the first floor of their historic Victorian into a full bathroom, including a beautifully tiled walk-in shower. He was so eager to show off his masterpiece. And, he promised Sarah he'd let the younger crew handle all the tall ladder climbing from now on.

Crystal Lake Gifts continued to benefit from the social media buzz around the Christmas Sweaters, and Trish introduced a full line of handknitted sweaters. Her online business had necessitated the addition of a full-time marketing coordinator and product manager. Trish shared with Kate that she'd finally achieved the business success she always promised herself she would.

It seems that Kate was still the person all the "girls" confided in. Trish also told Kate confidentially she and Derrick were expecting their first baby, but she wanted to wait until the next family dinner to tell everyone. The best part… the baby was due in late December.

Cassidy shared her intention to expand the inn with Peter and Amanda, who both enthusiastically supported the plan. They decided to include a spa in the new wing, and Amanda was excited to oversee both the design and operations, alongside her other duties. Having already met with the architect, Amanda was busy visiting various spas to gather ideas for creating the perfect spa setup for the inn. She told Kate, "Getting numerous massages is a tough job, but somebody has to do it and it might as well be me."

Dr. Foster and his family purchased a larger house to prepare for the arrival of their third child. They were adopting a newborn baby girl. Once they met her, it was love at first sight. They named her Ava.

Marie and her family visited the inn for a long weekend in February to pick up the Christmas quilt. Kate smiled to herself as she recalled how she retold the story of how Marie had arrived in a blizzard to get the Christmas quilt and ended up giving birth to a beautiful baby boy at the inn. They all toasted and cheered to the Christmas miracle.

Marie's grandmother fully recovered from the pneumonia she had around Christmas, but she wasn't able to handle the five-hour car ride from Boston to Lakeview. Instead, they connected via a video call. They walked her through the inn so she could see how it looked today and the changes it had gone through. They also showed her the playroom where the baby was born and where the fake wall was located that held the quilt-wrapped nativity scene.

Cassidy thoughtfully placed a plaque on the wall in the playroom, featuring a picture of the Christmas quilt and a brief explanation of how they'd discovered the quilt hidden in the wall—and now a picture of Marie's baby. They had a wonderful weekend, and the group decided that, even though they weren't related by blood, they were connected by special circumstances and the beautiful inn.

Of course, Kate continued to play a special role in Marie's life. They asked if their son could call her Auntie Kate when he was old enough to talk. That brought tears to her eyes.

Kate continued to contemplate her life, feeling amazed at how lucky she was. When Duncan had died, she'd thought her life was over, but she had to face it and not let it destroy her.

With the love of a good man and the support of her family and friends, she realized that the old saying was true—when one door closes, another one opens.

And she was perfectly content to now be back "home" at the Crystal Lake Inn, the perfect place in the ideal town, filled with love, interesting townspeople, and the best coffee in all of Maine. Somehow, Kate reflected, the inn brought people into each other's lives when they needed comfort or an inviting, maybe even magical, place to stay.

It was a prayer answered for Marie on a freezing winter night during a blizzard. When there was nowhere else to go, there was a room at the inn and special people to help rescue her, care for her, and keep her safe.

Crystal Lake Inn…truly, it's a magical place where miracles happen.

PS: Oh, and don't think I overlooked giving you the name of Marie's baby, born on Christmas, placed in a doll's bed, and swaddled in a handmade quilt. He was named… I'll leave that for you to decide!

Happy holidays to you and your loved ones from our family to yours.

ACKNOWLEDGMENTS

While writing is often a solitary effort, our stories and characters are frequently inspired by real-life experiences. We draw from experts, who surprisingly come from all age groups. Let me introduce the experts who contributed to this book.

The character Abby Roark, the Gold Medalist figure skater in this book, was inspired by my great-niece's love of figure skating. While I've changed her last name to protect her privacy, she provided the skating details. **Abby** has been skating for over seven years, has performed in multiple shows, and skates at the Fred Rust Ice Arena. She enjoys training for performances, and as a perfectionist, was happy to point out mistakes and incorrect terminology I used. Any remaining errors are mine alone. Abby and I share the common bond of being the middle child in our families. That makes us special (or independent and strong-willed, depending on how you see it)—sending hugs your way.

Karina Celeste DuPree, the Prima Ballerina, was inspired by another great-niece's love for dance and ballet. During performances, she seems to float across the stage, and while I might be a little biased, I believe she's a talented dancer.

In real life, **Karina** was named after a star, and she is always a star in our family. I also changed her name to protect this pre-teen from feedback on the many mistakes I probably made regarding the details of The Nutcracker ballet and the history of the art. I also included the name **Celeste** as a nod to our youngest family member. I'm so proud of you both—sending big hugs.

Finally, for those who know me well, you are aware that I have a deep love for quilts. I have quite an extensive collection — please don't ask how many, as it's embarrassing. However, I don't have the skills to make them myself.

Fortunately, I have a friend who not only makes stunning quilts but also teaches quilting and designs new patterns. **Catherine** Wilson has been an avid quilter since her teenage years, and later, she ventured into quilt design. What began as a hobby evolved into a flourishing career. She blends traditional piecing with a modern twist that honors the rich heritage of quilting while pushing the boundaries of modern expression.

Catherine contributed details about the antique quilt found at the inn. I'm fortunate to own a Friendship Quilt she made for me when we were expats in the UK over twenty years ago. Thank you, Cat, for your input and friendship over the years. You can see her work at *www.queeniequilts.com*.

TO MY READERS –
A NOTE FROM SUSAN

The publishing industry has undergone significant changes in the past decade, with more authors than ever finding innovative ways to connect with their readers. But none of this would be possible without you buying my books and leaving those valuable reviews.

Specifically, I want to thank everyone who has read one of my books—it means the world to me. And a very special thanks to those who have read all the books in the Crystal Lake Series. Although each book can be read independently, I love how the characters carry over from one book to the next. I often hear from readers who tell me how much they enjoy the fictional town of Lakeview, Maine, and desire to book a room at Crystal Lake Inn. I'd love to stay at the inn myself. I've combined the best features from places I've visited over the years into the inn that serves as the series' centerpiece.

I'm truly excited about Crystal Lake Christmas. The holidays are my favorite time of year, and I'm fortunate to have a family that celebrates the season, spends quality time together, and literally, always has room at the "inn" (or in our case, at The Farm) for friends and family.

Please take a moment to leave a review. Reviews are crucial for helping other readers decide if they'll enjoy this book. Just imagine, your review might inspire hundreds of readers to buy my book — something I would genuinely appreciate.

My books are available on Amazon and most online retailers. Visit my website for more details and links to independent bookstores that proudly sell my books. You can also send me a message through the Contact form on my website. This is the best way to invite me to join your book club via Zoom. These events are always a fun way to connect directly with my readers and for you to ask those burning questions behind the scenes.

Keep Reading!

https://www.amazon.com/stores/author/B09CBYDHHF
www.facebook.com/booksbysusanwgreen
www.booksbysusanwgreen.com

ABOUT THE AUTHOR

Susan **W. Green,** an award-winning author, delights readers with her charming, lighthearted romance novels filled with fun challenges, humor, and happy endings.

CRYSTAL LAKE CHRISTMAS is the third book in the CRYSTAL LAKE series. While each story stands on its own, you'll find your favorite characters making appearances across the series. Her debut novel, *Crystal Lake Inn,* earned an Independent Press Award and has been enjoyed by readers in eight different countries. Her second book, *Crystal Lake Gifts*, is the winner of the International Impact Book Award and continues to warm the hearts of her loyal readers.

After a fulfilling thirty-five-year career in banking, she enjoys a vibrant life beyond writing. You'll often see her collaborating with universities and women's organizations, serving on various boards, supporting entrepreneurs, mentoring others, or getting lost in a good book. She's also a coffee lover, so don't be surprised to find coffee sprinkled throughout her books—it's a little bit of her favorite treat in every story.

Susan and her husband live in Northern Maryland, where they cherish the peaceful countryside, love hosting family and friends, and enjoy sitting on the front porch with a good cup of coffee.